A WOMAN SCREAMED . . .

A circle had formed around the woman, who lay writhing on the floral carpet. Two people were trying to prevent her from hitting herself with her flailing arms. Most of the others seemed stunned into paralysis. The cup that had contained her punch lay shattered on the floor.

Suddenly, the woman's body arched—once, twice, three times until the spasms were coming so quickly her body was almost continuously in an arched-back position.

"Oh, no!" Someone gasped. "I think she stopped breathing!"

Other Iris House Mysteries by
Jean Hager
from Avon Books

BLOOMING MURDER

DEAD AND BURIED

AN IRIS HOUSE MYSTERY

JEAN HAGER

AVON BOOKS ◆ NEW YORK

DEAD AND BURIED is an original publication of Avon Books. This work has never before appeared in book form. This work is a novel. Any similarity to actual persons or events is purely coincidental.

AVON BOOKS
A division of
The Hearst Corporation
1350 Avenue of the Americas
New York, New York 10019

Copyright © 1995 by Jean Hager
Published by arrangement with the author
Library of Congress Catalog Card Number: 94-96556
ISBN: 0-380-77210-8

First Avon Books Printing: June 1995

AVON TRADEMARK REG. U.S. PAT. OFF. AND IN OTHER COUNTRIES, MARCA REGISTRADA, HECHO EN U.S.A.

Printed in the U.S.A.

RA   10 9 8 7 6 5 4 3 2

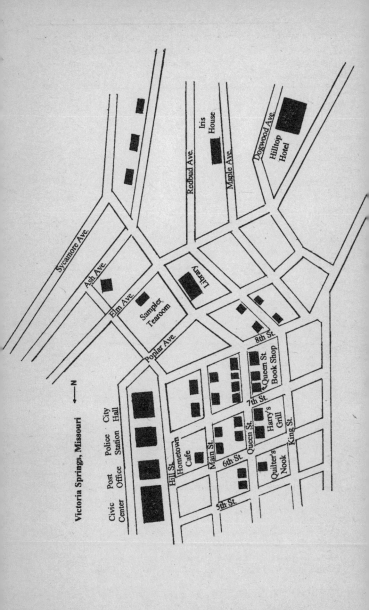

DEAD

AND

BURIED

Chapter 1

Rita De'Lane's glittering, sienna-nailed finger stabbed out the airline's number on the touch tone dial. Clutching the receiver to her ear, she paced across her apartment as far as the cord would stretch, spun around on one heel, and paced back again.

If she had been a cartoon, smoke would have been curling from her ears. As it was, she was angry enough to tear the phone from the wall. But that would be like getting mad at the cat and kicking the dog. And then she'd have to go out and use a pay phone.

She muttered an oath. *Blasted voice mail.* You could never get hold of a real person these days without first listening to this garbage and punching more buttons. She gave it ten years before every business in the city was run totally by computers. Human beings would be obsolete.

At the prompting of the recorded message, she hissed another purple curse and jabbed "2."

When a ticket agent finally answered, she barked, "So pleased you could bother with little old me."

"Ma'am?"

"Did you enjoy your lunch?"

"Pardon me?"

"Never mind." The jerk didn't even recognize sarcasm when he heard it. "How soon can you get me to Victoria Springs, Missouri?"

1

"Say again, ma'am."

"VICTORIA SPRINGS, MISSOURI!" she bellowed. "I have to get there right away. This is an emergency."

"We don't fly into Victoria Springs, ma'am."

Great. It figured.

"What's the nearest city?" the agent asked.

"How the hell should I know! Look it up."

"One moment, please."

Rita tapped her foot furiously. Leave it to Francine, Rita's temperamental-writer client, to hole up in the boondocks where there wasn't even an airport. Well, it would take more brainpower than Francine Alexander possessed to outwit Rita De'Lane. After Rita had struck out with Francine's editor and her landlord, she had gone to Francine's apartment building last night and questioned neighbors until she found one who knew where Francine had disappeared to.

A high school reunion. Were it anyone but Francine, Rita wouldn't believe it. But it sounded like the sort of hokey affair that Francine would love.

Rita hadn't slept a wink all night. This morning, exhausted but determined, she'd called her secretary at home and instructed her to phone every hotel, motel, and bed-and-breakfast inn in Victoria Springs until she found the one where Francine was staying, then make her a reservation at the same place. Fortunately, they'd had a last-minute room cancellation beginning Monday. Rita would sleep in a rental car until then if necessary.

The secretary had been outraged that Rita would call her on a Saturday. Rita had apologized profusely. Good secretaries were hard to find, and Rita thought she'd pushed the woman about as far as she dared. Which was why she was dealing with the airline herself.

While she listened to canned music, Rita paced and drove sharp-nailed fingers through her short, boyishly cut hair. The style was the latest "rave" among successful professional women, according to her hairdresser, who had charged her all four limbs to do it.

The sixty-five-year-old superintendent of Rita's apartment building, however, had been amazed. He said it looked just like the burr cut he'd worn as a boy. "Everybody wore 'em back then," he'd said. "The *boys*, I mean. Easiest haircut I ever had. Combed it with a washrag."

The ticket agent came back. "That would be Springfield."

Rita had never heard of Springfield, either. As far as she was concerned, everything west of the Hudson River was wasteland. And her contempt for small towns was matched only by her contempt for temperamental authors.

"Can you get me there today? I'll rent a car at the airport."

"Where will you be departing from?"

"New York City."

More canned music. It made Rita want to pull out what was left of her hair. Evidently, the whole world was terrified of silence.

Then, "I'm sorry, but those weekend flights are fully booked. I can get you on a morning flight out of New York on Monday."

Rita scorched the agent's ears with several more unladylike words from her extensive repertoire.

He remained unruffled. Maybe he was a computer, too. "Would you like me to put you on the waiting list for a Sunday flight?" Why should he care? *He* didn't have to get the hell and gone to Victoria Springs, Missouri, to save his career.

Rita took a few deep breaths to calm herself. It wasn't the stupid reservation clerk's fault. "No, I'll go Monday. What's your earliest flight?" On the bright side, she wouldn't have to sleep in a car.

Her flight and a rental car reserved, Rita called the head of the literary agency she worked for and left word on *his* voice mail that an emergency had arisen and she would be out of the office for a few days. Let him wonder where she'd gone.

After Rita had worked her butt off for the agency, the

ingrate had called her into his office Friday afternoon to say rumors were circulating that their best-selling author Francine Alexander was leaving the agency. Rita had already heard the rumors, but she had been hoping they wouldn't reach her boss's ears. He actually *liked* Francine.

The little turd kept shaking his head at the dire thought of Francine's leaving, his fat jowls jiggling as he talked. He'd hinted that if the rumors were true, Rita's position at the agency could be in jeopardy.

She lit a cigarette and puffed furiously. Was there no loyalty left in this rotten, stinking world?

She had reminded her boss of her ten years of faithful service. The lard-butt had leaned back in his chair, folded his pudgy hands on his ballooning stomach and, with a tight little smile, asked, "But what have you done for us lately, Rita?"

Very funny.

And how *dare* that egotistical space cadet Francine even think of dumping her for another agent. Francine Alexander was a no-talent hack who'd gotten lucky with her first book. It happened sometimes that a mediocre book touched a chord with a large segment of the reading public. Like a bolt of lightning, it couldn't be predicted; there was no rhyme or reason to it. Of course, the author who was struck by the lightning always thought it was no more than her due; *finally* her talent had been recognized.

No matter. Once a book made the major best-seller lists, the author was assured of good sales on the next book or two. Name recognition alone would move books for a while. After that, if readers became disenchanted they'd turn against a writer as quickly as they'd embraced the author in the first place. Like a rabid dog turns on its master. It had begun to happen with that ghastly third book of Francine's, but meanwhile Rita and her agency had made a tub full of commission money from their cut of Francine's royalties.

About a month ago, Francine had told Rita that the book

she was working on now was going to catapult her back to the top.

Catapult. Sometimes Francine got carried away.

Rita had pressed for details, but Francine had been very mysterious about the story line, saying only that it was the book she'd wanted to write all her life. Not a peep about being dissatisfied with Rita's work as Francine's agent, the wimp.

Rita hadn't heard from Francine since, and then the rumors had started circulating through the city's small, inbred publishing community that Francine Alexander was unhappy with her current representation and had been interviewing agents.

Francine hadn't written anything publishable in a good while, and it was more than likely that this work-in-progress would turn out to be another bomb. If that were the case, no agency in the world could save her. She would be just another literary has-been. But if it turned out to be the blockbuster Francine predicted, it could make the agency, and Francine's agent, very, very rich.

Rita couldn't afford to count Francine out.

She took a deep drag on her cigarette. Damnit, the woman had a contract. Unfortunately, agency contracts were broken all the time. Agencies gave lip service to the gentlemanly notion that if a writer was unhappy they didn't want to stand in the way of the author going to another agency. In most cases, agent and writer shook hands, metaphorically speaking, and the writer moved on. But in the case of a best-selling author, agencies weren't so gentlemanly.

Rita wasn't going to give up without a fight. She intended to hold Francine's feet to the fire on this one.

"Damn betcha!" she muttered and smashed the stub of her cigarette in the nearest ash tray to emphasize the point.

Who'd nursed Francine through scathing reviews and rejected proposals and even writer's block? Who'd lied through her teeth, when Francine was immobilized by self-doubt, and assured her that she was a fine writer?

Who'd performed the miracle of getting a decent advance on that third novel, which would never have been published if several markers hadn't been called in?

None other than Rita De'Lane!

Chapter 2

Rachel Leander Waller hesitated beneath the street lamp at the corner of King Street and Eighth, stretching out her legs. When she ran, she was sensually aware of her body, its bones, ligaments, and muscles, its smooth efficiency, but her mind hummed along in neutral. When her thoughts clicked into gear again, she sometimes felt disoriented. Which was how she felt right now.

When she left Iris House, the elegant bed and breakfast where she was staying, she'd had no intention of wandering, in her solitary nocturnal jog through Victoria Springs, to King Street. But, suddenly it seemed, she was there—as if she'd been guided by some hidden sensor.

It was after midnight. Everything was silent and strange in the moonlight. A faint breeze, carrying the scent of honeysuckle, cooled her bare legs and rustled the leaves of a sycamore tree on the corner.

The house where she had lived until she was seventeen was the next-to-last house at the far end of the block. She could not see it from where she stood, but its presence drifted to her like a noxious cloud.

Even though the June night was mild and her T-shirt was damp with perspiration, she shivered from an interior chill. Above her, moths and june bugs circled the street lamp, irresistibly drawn to the light that could easily destroy them. Were they driven by the same incomprehensible compulsion that pulled her toward the house at the other end of the block?

She had visited her mother and younger sister a dozen times since her marriage, but she had not been on King Street since the day, more than twenty years ago, the three of them had moved into a cramped, two-bedroom apartment near the center of town. Her mother and Jane still lived in that apartment, and each time Rachel saw it, the walls of the four rooms seemed to have moved closer together since her previous visit.

Although the activities scheduled for the twenty-year reunion of her high school class didn't begin until next Monday, Rachel had arrived in Victoria Springs yesterday, Friday, to spend time with her mother and sister.

Her mother had taken it for granted that Rachel would stay at the apartment and had set up a cot in the living room. Rachel had waited as long as she dared to reveal that she'd reserved a room at Iris House and would check in there Saturday afternoon.

She'd be in the way, she'd said; she didn't want to be a bother. Her mother didn't care about Rachel's reasons, she was hurt. Rachel had been afraid of that. But the alternative was worse because not wanting to inconvenience her mother and sister was only half the truth. The other half was that she wasn't sure how the memories stirred by the reunion would affect her, and she needed a private retreat if she felt overwhelmed.

Fortunately her husband, Brent, had not questioned her reasons for wanting to attend the reunion alone. It was an inconvenient time for him to be away from his work, in any case, and their daughters, aged nine and eleven, were enrolled in a day camp next week.

She could, of course, have avoided the issue altogether by sending her regrets, as she had for the ten-year reunion. But the intervening years had given her perspective, if nothing else; and even weeks ago when the invitation had arrived, she'd known she had to come this time. They would all be here—Rachel, Francine, Barry, and Ted. The Four Musketeers, their classmates had dubbed them.

In this place, with the four of them together again, she hoped to prove, once and for all, that the past they had shared in this small Missouri town could no longer touch her. It was a very different past from the one she had described to Brent and her daughters.

But the past was dead. Now she must bury it. They'd had a saying in high school when they goofed up: A hundred years from now nobody will know the difference. It hadn't been a hundred years, but twenty was too long to live with what-ifs.

A june bug hit the street lamp and stuck there, flapping frantically. The sizzle of the frying insect was amazingly loud in the silence before it dropped to the sidewalk. Rachel stared at the dead bug, thinking how fragile life was. And how final, death.

She shook off the despondency that had gripped her and, loosening the sleeves of the light jacket she'd tied around her waist, she slipped it on over her T-shirt.

Hesitantly at first, and then with more determined steps, she started down King Street toward Seventh Street.

It was, after all, only a house.

There were no lights in any of the houses on the block, but street lamps kept her from stumbling on the cracked and buckled sidewalk. The neighborhood had been neatly middle-class twenty years ago, but now the impression she received was one of creeping deterioration. Her mother had said that the old neighborhood was populated mostly by renters now, their former neighbors had moved to newer houses on the edges of town.

Halfway down the block, she passed the red-brick bungalow where Megan and Marilyn Johansen had lived, freckle-faced twins three years younger than Rachel. She had taught them to lead cheers. Rachel smiled wistfully at the memory. She hoped they'd made the squad.

There, across the street, was the Perkins's house, a two-story with white shingles and green shutters. Light from the pole lamp in the yard revealed that several of the shutters were missing. Such neglect would not have been countenanced during the Perkins's tenure. Mr. Perkins had kept the house in tip-top shape and maintained the yard like a garden. Mrs. Perkins had loved to bake and had often walked across the street with cookies or a cake for the Leanders.

But that had been twenty years ago. The Perkins had been in their late sixties even then. It was unlikely they were still living. She wondered who owned the house now. An absentee landlord, probably, who didn't want to spend money on repairs.

With some reluctance, Rachel turned from the Perkins's house. A few more steps brought her to the old-fashioned frame structure that had been her childhood home: living room, dining room and kitchen downstairs, and three bedrooms upstairs, with a single bathroom off the downstairs hall.

Painted white when the Leanders had lived there, it seemed darker now though she couldn't identify the color at night. Gray, perhaps. Like her mother's apartment, the house looked much smaller than she remembered. She wondered if its ghosts had shrunk, too.

Rachel's heart thudded.

Overgrown shrubbery hid the porch railing, or the place where the railing had been. Even at night, the house gave off an aura of disrepair. Perhaps the railing had been removed when it needed painting and was never replaced. It was hard to tell with all that shrubbery. She had an illogical impulse to venture up the front walk far enough to check. But what did it matter, really, if the whole house had collapsed? She almost wished it had, for after all these years it still seemed to embody the past she was determined to put behind her; and she knew she could not go up that walk if her life depended on it.

A spider of anxiety crawled down her neck.

No. She wouldn't give in to irrational fear. Nobody she knew had lived here for twenty years.

It was only a house.

The impotent fury and sick guilt she was feeling were merely old emotions, dredged to the surface by the class reunion. But she could control her mind. She had done so for twenty years. It had saved her sanity.

Still, all the control she could muster did not fully disperse the chill wind of fear that seemed to be blowing through her. She should not have come here alone, in the middle of the night. Safer to bury the past in the full light of day.

She had to get hold of herself. With a defiant lift of her chin she gave herself a little shake.

She could hear the low hum of an automobile engine a block or two away. A teenager driving his girl home after a date? As Ted had driven her so long ago. How would it feel, seeing Ted again? And the others?

She glanced back at the house one last time. Then quickly, her heart pounding, Rachel ran back to the end of the block. When she reached the corner, she felt a near-uncontrollable urge to look over her shoulder, but she mastered it and kept her eyes ahead.

It had all happened in another lifetime.

She wouldn't think about it.

Leaving King Street behind, she jogged up the hill toward Iris House.

Chapter 3

Though the mills of God grind slowly, yet they grind exceeding small.

Albert Butterfield's mother used to tell him that when he came home bruised and crying after a bully's beating, which happened with terrifying frequency as he was growing up. He'd been a sickly child, easily cowed, and a scrawny teenager with glasses and pimples, often the brunt of jokes by his peers. An IQ of 150 had cut no ice among the student body of Victoria Springs High School in the 1970s, and he doubted that things had changed all that much in the '90s.

Where his mother had picked up that mills-of-God saying was something of a mystery. Perhaps she'd heard it from one of her customers at the beauty shop. At the time, Albert hadn't understood what it meant. When he finally figured it out, he'd preferred the more modern: What goes around comes around. That philosophy had seen him through high school, and his grade point average and SAT scores had won him a full scholarship at Northwestern.

That morning, Sunday, Albert had flown to Springfield where he'd rented the biggest car available, a red Lincoln Town Car. He would have preferred arriving in one of the three Mercedes-Benzes he owned. Two of them were in Chicago, his principal residence, the third in Kansas City where he kept a penthouse apartment. But he'd left from Chicago, and he couldn't spare the time for such a long drive.

He hadn't been back to Victoria Springs for sixteen years, but he wasn't surprised by the changes he saw, since he knew the once-sleepy little town had become something of a tourist mecca.

Not on the scale of Branson, thank God, but even here Ozark crafts and country music seemed to be the main draws. The old Hilltop Hotel had been remodeled, a new conference wing added. Shops selling homespun crafts and cheap souvenirs lined the streets of the business district, and bed and breakfasts were everywhere.

After checking around, his secretary, Glenda, had concluded that the most desirable accommodations were to be had at Iris House, which it turned out was the old Darcy family home. Somehow Glenda had discovered that the four musketeers had reservations there, and she had taken the last available room for Albert. He had to admit his accommodations were first-class.

At the moment, Albert was stretched out there in his jockey shorts, spread-eagle on a white-canopied four-poster bed.

He scratched his soft belly and looked around him with a supercilious lift of tan brows. The Carnaby Room. Named for an iris whose rose-red falls were edged in pink. Albert knew this because the iris was depicted in a painting on the wall with the words "The Carnaby Iris" beneath it. Personally, Albert didn't give a tinker's damn about irises. He didn't waste his time on hobbies; he preferred to spend it making money.

The plush carpet was the same rose-red color as the iris and the wallpaper and draperies were sprinkled with rose, pink, and blue tulips. Every guest room in the remodeled Victorian house was named for an iris, it seemed.

Too cute by half for Albert's tastes, but he could tolerate it for a few days, considering how much fun he was going to have.

A gloating smile curved his thin lips as he gazed up at the snowy canopy. He felt like General MacArthur. *I shall return.* It had taken twenty years but, like MacArthur, Albert had finally come back in triumph to the scene of his past humiliation.

Yes, indeed. What goes around comes around. His sole purpose in rearranging his busy schedule to attend this dinky high school reunion was to impress that truth indelibly upon the inferior brains of his former classmates.

Especially the Four Musketeers. Belonging to their popular clique had been his major teenage fantasy. Specifically, he had dreamed of being Ted Ponte, the football captain who'd gone steady with Rachel Leander, homecoming queen, cheerleader, prettiest girl in school. Alas, even a genius is subject to the herd instinct during his formative years.

Albert sat up with a grunt and dug in a pocket of his Gucci suitcase for the folder his secretary had handed him as he left his Chicago office. It contained the background checks he'd requested. A cardinal rule of Albert's was never to approach any situation without being thoroughly prepared. That guiding principle had been an important factor in his business success. In a dozen years, he had built a multimillion-dollar high-tech corporation with offices all over the globe, and plans were afoot to announce an initial public offering of the company's shares in the fall.

He leafed through the sheets in the folder, acquainting himself with the histories of Rachel Leander Waller, Francine Alexander, Ted Ponte, and Barry Wilhelm since their graduation from Victoria Springs High School.

Rachel had dropped out of college in her junior year to marry Brent Waller and put him through law school. She had never returned to school for her degree.

Rachel's husband, Brent Waller, was a partner in a Topeka law firm where he handled corporate clients of middling importance. The Wallers had two young daughters, Tiffany and Amanda. The senior class prophesy, published in the high school newspaper twenty years ago, had predicted that Rachel would become a film star or a model.

The prophesy could not have been further off the mark. The girl of his teenage dreams had turned out to be disappointingly middle-class. Rachel was an ordinary suburban housewife. Probably belonged to the Junior League and the PTA, Albert thought with a snort of contempt. With her looks, she could have had it all.

"You traded your birthright for a mess of pottage, Rachel," he mumbled as he laid the first sheet of paper aside and picked up the second.

Francine had done a little better for herself. Her personal life hadn't come to much—she was twice divorced with no children. But she was a minor professional success. Eight years ago, she'd published a sappy, sentimental romance novel, *Passion's Purple Blooms*, that had surprised the industry by rising to the Number 2 spot on the *New York Times* best-seller list and staying there for three months. Albert had tried to read the book to see what all the fuss was about, but he couldn't get through the turgid prose of the first chapter. How it had made the prestigious *Times* list remained unfathomable.

He could only conclude there were amazing numbers of silly, idle women in the world who had nothing better to do than to read such drivel. Come to think of it, his mother, now living in an Arkansas retirement community, had read the book and raved about it.

Francine had published two novels since. Both had been universally panned by critics. One had stayed at Number 8 on the *Times* list for three weeks, then dropped to Number 10 for a couple more weeks. The last one hadn't even made the top ten, but had hovered at fourteen or fifteen for a week or two, then sank like a brick. The publisher's returns on the last book had been disastrously high, and Albert had read with fiendish delight in *Publishers Weekly* that it had turned down Francine's last three book proposals.

Poor Franny must be feeling pretty desperate about now. The thought elicited an evil chuckle from Albert.

He picked up the next sheet of paper. Ted Ponte had

played college football and been drafted by a pro team, but had sat out his first season on the bench. An injury in his second year had put an abrupt end to any chance he might have had at a successful professional career.

After leaving the pros, Ted had borrowed from relatives and put a second mortgage on his home to buy a sporting goods store that he then proceeded to run straight into bankruptcy.

He'd married his college sweetheart the summer after their graduation, and they had one son. The couple had divorced three years ago, and the boy lived with his mother in Dallas. For the past few years, Ted had been selling insurance in Houston. An ignominious end for Victoria Springs's star football player of the '70s.

Albert caught a glimpse of his long-jawed, shrewd-eyed face in the mirror. His expression was an odd mixture of reflection and smugness as he turned away and laid Ted's sheet aside.

To think he'd have given anything, as a teenager, to *be* Ted Ponte. Every night he'd prayed that he'd wake up the next morning and find himself magically transformed into the 180-pound footballer. Yes, he'd actually done that, though remembering it embarrassed him.

Now look at the two of them. If he were still a praying man, he'd fall on his knees and thank God for withholding the miracle.

The next background report was longer than the others. Since Barry Wilhelm was something of a public figure in Missouri, he was occasionally mentioned in the newspapers, usually for his positions on various political issues. Copies of several of the articles were included with the file. Albert scanned them. Clearly, Barry had mastered the politician's art of sounding intelligent and articulate without really saying anything.

Barry had married Adeline Van Brunt of Savannah, Georgia, shortly after graduating from the University of Missouri, and they had a son and daughter. Barry had been a state legislator for twelve years and was now running for the U.S. Senate. The incumbent, who had held the seat for twenty-eight years, was retiring.

Recently, one of Barry's aides had contacted Albert's Chicago office to inquire if "Representative Wilhelm's old high school chum" would consider sponsoring a Kansas City campaign fund-raiser. Albert had taken devilish joy in declining—through his secretary, of course.

He had relished dictating the words: Mr. Butterfield regretted to say that he would be involved in important business negotiations for the foreseeable future and would have no time for less pressing matters.

Albert had, however, found time to make a sizable contribution to Barry's opponent.

"Old school chum, my arse," he sneered. It had been Barry who'd come up with a twist on Albert's surname and hung the appellation "Butterface" on him, a cruel allusion to his oily complexion. And Butterface he'd remained to the end of his days at Victoria Springs High. It was even worse when Barry was with his girlfriend, Francine, because she always cackled shrilly at Barry's every juvenile attempt at humor.

Albert could still feel his blood pressure rise when he thought of the pain he'd endured at the hands of his classmates. And Barry and Francine had been the instigators.

Could Barry actually be so dense as to think Albert remembered him fondly? Incredible as it seemed to Albert, it was possible. Barry had never been known for his sensitivity.

He turned the sheet over and saw a fifth sheet in the file. Puzzled, he picked it up and read the name at the top. Robert "Bobby" Van Brunt Wilhelm. Barry's fifteen-year-old son.

He read the profile with increasing interest. Bobby Wilhelm had caused quite a bit of havoc in his short lifetime. He must be driving his parents crazy. Imagine Barry Wilhelm, good student, high school student-body president, big man on campus at UM, and Adeline Van Brunt, Savannah debutante and stereotypical sorority girl, trying to cope with a son like Bobby.

The daughter was not mentioned. She must be the conforming type.

Albert slapped the folder shut with a ferocious grin. Hot damn, he was going to enjoy himself at this reunion. At last he could deal with all of them from a position of superior strength.

Physical attractiveness and athletic ability counted for little in the real world. Money and power. That's what mattered, and if you had enough money, the power followed automatically. In an article last year, *Forbes* had said that Albert exuded power. He liked that.

And he was going to make sure they all knew it before this reunion was over.

Zero hour approached.

He'd already laid out his clothes. A pair of B. Beltrami shoes, a heather gray Armani jacket—and an inspired touch of insouciance, faded jeans.

He would give them time to gather before he made a casual entrance. It was the kind of subtle statement that appealed to him. The last person to arrive at any function was usually the most important. Not that there would be any doubt here about who that was, no matter when he arrived.

Now, where had he put that confounded invitation? It was on the bedside table when he checked in. He got off the bed and moved the table out from the wall. There it was. It had fallen down between the table and the bed. He held up the gold-engraved white square and read:

Please join your fellow guests
for tea in the library
Sunday, 3—4 p.m.
Take the circular staircase
at the east end of
the second floor hall.

Tess Darcy,
Proprietor

Had Albert needed any further proof that he was a long way from Chicago, this frilly bit of paper would have provided it.

A damned tea party. *How nauseatingly quaint.*

Chapter 4

Freshly showered and attired in a kelly green cotton top, yellow skirt and yellow sandals, Tess surveyed the lace-draped tea table. She had placed it by the floor-to-ceiling windows that formed the curving west wall of the tower room. The draperies were open, but filmy white undercurtains filtered the afternoon sunlight, transforming brilliant yellow rays into a soft amber glow.

The diffused light sparkled on the silver tea and coffee service, the sterling flatware lined up beside lace-edged linen napkins, the hand-painted china created specially for Iris House. The irises decorating each plate and cup were the color of ripe raspberries.

Crystal serving plates held currant and pecan scones, meringue kisses, grilled marmalade fingers, and thin slices of lemon ginger pound cake. The silver pots filled with vanilla-almond coffee and orange-spice tea sat ready.

Having satisfied herself that everything was done, Tess heaved a huge sigh and dropped into the nearest wicker chair. She was so tired.

Gertie Bogart, the Iris House cook, had warned Tess when she opened the bed and breakfast that regular Sunday afternoon teas might prove to be too much, with all the other duties inherent in running a bed and breakfast.

Luke Fredrik had protested even louder than Gertie since Luke had countless ideas of more pleasant ways for Tess to spend her Sundays. Tess closed her eyes and, for an instant, indulged in recalling the last time she'd been with Luke. The memory made her skin tingle with warmth. Dear Luke did have such *wonderful* ideas.

With a reluctant sigh, she pulled her mind back to the present. To some extent, Gertie and Luke had been right about the teas. Sundays were exhausting.

Since Gertie didn't work on Sundays, Tess always served a continental breakfast, offering a variety of croissants, rolls, and muffins from a local bakery. Often, she barely managed to clear the dining room table and clean up the kitchen in time to begin preparations for the Sunday afternoon Victorian tea. Of course, Gertie had prepared food in advance. Still, Tess had to lay the table, carry up the food and dishes, serve her guests, and clean up afterward. She had often wished that her Grandfather Darcy had installed a dumbwaiter when he built the house, which Tess had inherited last year from her late Aunt Iris. She had promptly quit her job as an office manager for a large law firm in Atlanta, moved to Victoria Springs, and spent the rest of her inheritance and her own savings to renovate the house, fulfilling a long-held dream of owning a bed and breakfast.

It was a lot of work, but Tess didn't regret her decision. Nor was she ready to abandon the Sunday teas. She enjoyed the weekly gatherings in the library. Not only did they introduce her guests to the library, but she got to know them better and it allowed them to meet each other in a more leisurely setting than at breakfast.

It wasn't often that her guests knew each other prior to their stay at Iris House, as was the case with the people who were in town to attend their high school class reunion. She wasn't sure about one of the guests, though, the one who was scheduled to arrive tomorrow—Rita De'Lane of New York City. Ms. De'Lane's secretary had made the reservation, and Tess hadn't had a chance to ask if she was coming for the reunion. Gertie hadn't recognized the name, though, and Gertie knew virtually everyone who'd lived in Victoria Springs for the past forty years.

Although the Darcys were one of Victoria Springs's old families, and Tess's Aunt Dahlia, Uncle Maurice, and cousin Hyacinthe had lived there all their lives, Tess's father had not returned after his college graduation. Thus, in spite of the Darcy name Tess was still something of an outsider. To gain acceptance with the locals, she had joined the garden club, an organization so highly regarded in Victoria Springs that it was referred to simply as The Club, and the quilters's guild. She was still a novice at both gardening and quilting, but Aunt Dahlia was always available to advise her on the upkeep of the Iris gardens surrounding Iris House and she had recently enrolled in a beginning quilting class at a local shop, The Quilter's Nook.

From her wicker chair, Tess admired the four sections of bookcases that faced the windows. The first section was devoted to nonfiction, the second to general fiction, the third to mystery and suspense novels, and the fourth to science fiction and romance. Tess had rearranged a shelf in the last section, temporarily displacing her favorite romance authors, Genell Dellin and Johanna Lindsey in order to shelve Francine Alexander's three hardcover romance novels at eye level.

The most recently published, *Love's Lusty Lady*, had been difficult to find. According to Tess's cousin, Hyacinthe, manager of the Queen Street Book Shop, the novel had already been remaindered by the publisher and was no longer stocked by any of the wholesalers. Cinny had finally tracked one down through a book-search company that had charged Tess twice the cover price. She'd agreed only because she thought it would be a nice touch to have Francine's books in the library during her visit. Some of the other guests may wish to read them, though Cinny had advised Tess in confidence not to waste her time.

"The last one's the worst of the three," Cinny had said with the lift of a delicately arched blond eyebrow, "and that's saying quite a lot."

In spite of Cinny's poor opinion of Francine Alexander's literary ability, she was having an autograph party for the novelist Tuesday afternoon in connection with the class reunion. "The woman called me herself to request a signing," Cinny had told Tess. "What was I supposed to say? Besides, she's local. That always sells books."

Tess and Cinny's mother, Dahlia, had spent the past two days helping Cinny prepare for the signing which was why Tess was even more tired than usual this Sunday. They'd moved furniture and an entire section of books in Cinny's shop to make room for the refreshment table and the small Queen Anne desk and chair where Francine would sign her novels. Since Francine was a native of Victoria Springs, Cinny expected to sell several hundred books and had ordered accordingly—a hardcover of the first novel and paperback reprint copies of the other two.

Tess covered a yawn and glanced at her watch. Five minutes before three. Guests would begin arriving any time. To keep from falling asleep, she stood and plumped chair and sofa cushions, which were upholstered in an attractive chintz fabric featuring purple daisies, pink irises, and bright green foliage vining across a white background that matched the white wicker furniture. She had only recently replaced the old upholstery and the outer draperies, which were of the same spring-like fabric.

The library was one of Tess's favorite rooms, particularly when she could have it to herself and had the time to curl up with a book. Which didn't happen as often as she would like these days.

Hearing footsteps on the wrought iron staircase leading to the library, Tess smoothed her curly auburn hair and turned toward the door.

"Don't make me laugh, Adeline. You can switch that Southern charm on and off like a faucet, not that you can be bothered to waste it on me any more." State Representative Barry Wilhelm's tense, irritated voice floated clearly up the spiral staircase to the library's open doorway, where Tess stood.

"Oooh, poor mistreated baby," Adeline crooned, her voice dripping with sarcasm.

"Don't misunderstand me. If I had my way, I'd never have to witness that gentle Southern lady act of yours again. I know the real woman beneath it is about as gentle as a pit-bull dog. But it has its uses. Just be sure the charm's turned on when *he's* around."

"I may not feel like being charming," Adeline snapped. "I'm not your windup toy, you know. And I didn't want to come to this asinine high school reunion in the first place."

"I suggested you stay at home, but you had to get a look at my high school girlfriend. Afraid we might fan the embers of that old flame during the reunion?"

"Shut up, Barry. Just shut up."

"Look, I know this isn't much fun for you. But you *will* lay on the charm. I need big bucks for a media blitz the last two weeks before the election. *He* could make a few phone calls and, in thirty minutes's time, fund the whole media campaign. So you'll charm him because you want to go to Washington as much as I do."

"There is that. If I don't get out of stodgy old Jefferson City soon, I'll simply die of boredom." Adeline's deep Southern drawl had turned whiny. "Whatever would you do without me, Barry dear?"

Obviously the couple didn't dream they could be heard in the library. Tess moved quickly across the room to a window and was standing with her back to the door, looking out, when the Wilhelms entered.

Adeline was looking over her shoulder at her husband. "Damnit, Barry, I told you we were early. Nobody's here yet—oh, Miss Darcy"—the tone changed from sharp to saccharine in an eye's blink when she saw Tess—"there you are."

Tess turned from the window with a warm, welcoming

smile. She'd learned to deal with difficult guests by reacting as if their petty complaints and grouchy moods were perfectly reasonable. "Please call me Tess, Mrs. Wilhelm."

"Bless your heart." She drew out "heart," made it into a two-syllable word. "Isn't that sweet of you? And you must call me Adeline." She was a slim woman in a baby blue silk dress as soft and delicate as a cloudless summer sky. The shimmering white collar tied in a big bow in the center of the low "v" made Tess think of debutante teas in the deep South of two generations ago. Adeline's rich chestnut hair was twisted smoothly into an intricate design at the back of her head, fine wisps left to curl with artful casualness around her oval face. Filtered sunlight trapped in the diamonds on ear lobes and fingers sparkled as she crossed the room, somehow giving the impression of a queen deigning to notice a poor, groveling peasant.

Adeline's husband, attired in an oatmeal-colored sport jacket with an open-collared, cream silk shirt and tan slacks, was a burly, blunt-featured man with a wide, friendly smile. His public face, Tess thought, confident it didn't match the one he'd worn when she heard him on the stairs.

"Oooo, look, dawh-lin'." Adeline swept a slender hand toward the tea table. Her Southern drawl had become more pronounced, now that she had an audience other than her husband. "Isn't this absolutely chaw-min?"

"Charming," Barry echoed and flashed incredibly white teeth at Tess. Capped, she'd wager.

"Sunday afternoon teas. What a perfectly genteel idea," Adeline said. "It reminds me of mah childhood in Savannah."

"Savannah's a lovely city," Tess said.

"Isn't it." Adeline consulted her slim gold wristwatch, a little frown marring her smooth, ivory brow. "We seem to be early."

"Actually, you're right on time," Tess assured her.

"My daw-lin husband has a penchant for punctuality."
She patted Barry's cheek and smiled up at him.

What a performance, Tess thought. "The others should
be arriving any second," she said. "In fact, I think I hear
someone on the stairs now."

Chapter 5

Seconds later, Rachel Waller stepped into the library, halting as her gray eyes swept over the three faces turned toward her. She wore a simple black-and-white checked cotton dress; on her it looked positively chic. Her waving ash-blond hair formed a soft frame for her face. She had a slender, fit runner's body and wore a modicum of makeup. But she was blessed with a natural beauty that needed no embellishments.

In that first instant, she seemed to brace herself to run a gauntlet; but when Barry Wilhelm cried, "Rachel!" and bounded toward her with arms outstretched, her taut face rearranged itself into a smile.

"Barry," she exclaimed as they embraced. "How wonderful to see you."

He held her at arm's length. "I swear, you're prettier than ever. And you don't look a day older than you did in high school, Rachel."

"You always were a kidder, Barry. But look at *you*. Why, you look—"

He interrupted with another laugh. "Don't say *I* haven't aged." He waggled a finger at her. "You can go to the bad place for lying, same as stealing, you know." He turned to his wife. "Rachel, I'd like you to meet my wonderful spouse, Adeline."

Barry's wonderful spouse had not stopped studying

Rachel with cool, calculating eyes since she'd stepped through the doorway. "So you're Rachel," she said now with a coquettish glance at her husband. "I've heard *so* much about you from Barry."

Rachel's eyes became guarded as the women shook hands, and she looked uncertainly from Adeline to Barry. "Nothing too scandalous, I trust." She managed a social smile that did not hide the vulnerability in the faint curve of her gentle mouth.

"Perish the thought, Rachel. Any teenage high jinks you had a hand in, I was in up to my neck," Barry said. "I'd be a fool to implicate myself, wouldn't I?"

Tess would have had to be unconscious to miss the undercurrents of unspoken meanings in the room. Some of the tenseness left Rachel's body. "That's true. We did get up to some pretty naughty tricks."

"Naughty." Barry said the word as if he were unsure of its meaning. But his faintly confused look faded so quickly that Tess wondered if she'd imagined it. "Remember the Friday night the two of us and Francine and Ted hauled that stinking goat through a window at the high school and left it in the principal's office?" Barry asked. "By Monday morning, the whole high school reeked of billy goat."

"Do I remember! I'll never forget that smell."

"And remember old Art Chamberlain getting on the P.A. system—" Barry turned to his wife for an explanatory aside. "Chamberlain was the high school principal." He turned back to Rachel. "Remember old Art announcing to the whole school that classes would not be dismissed, that we'd all have to suffer the consequences of a few students' irresponsible actions."

"We were lucky," Rachel put in, "that he never found out who did it."

"Yeah, hard as old Art tried. Remember how he always got that red spot between his eyes when he was mad. After he found the goat, the red spot was there for a full week."

"Poor man," Rachel said.

Then they laughed at the shared memory and, for a few

moments, Rachel seemed to relax. But the odd mixture of uncertainty and anxiety in her gray eyes remained. Tess could see the woman was definitely worried about something, and, remembering Barry's confusion, she wondered if the teenage high jinks Barry had mentioned included sexual encounters with Rachel. Perhaps Rachel feared Barry had confessed them to his wife.

If so, the atmosphere could be strained in Iris House while Rachel and Adeline were in residence. Unfortunately, people sometimes tried to recapture their lost youth at class reunions. Rachel, at least, had had the good sense to leave her husband at home.

But, wait . . . Hadn't Gertie said that Rachel dated Ted Ponte in high school while Barry had been paired with Francine Alexander?

Yet there was something almost proprietary in Barry's attitude toward Rachel. Perhaps he'd had a crush on Rachel in high school and meant to make up for lost time at the reunion. Well, if that's what Barry Wilhelm had in mind, it wasn't Tess's concern. She had enough to do without refereeing conflicts between her guests.

Quick, heavy steps sounded on the spiral staircase, and then Ted Ponte appeared on the landing. His eyes found Rachel immediately and he stepped into the room and grabbed her in a bear hug. And bear was the right word, Tess thought. Ted Ponte was well over six feet tall, while Rachel was barely five-four. And he must weigh over two hundred pounds. He was once a pro football player, Gertie had told Tess.

Though his well-tailored green sport jacket did a fair job of disguising it, the athlete's muscles were turning to fat as he approached forty. With his long arms wrapped around Rachel, his body appeared to swallow her, making her look smaller and more fragile.

She was smiling and her face was flushed as he dropped his arms and stepped back. "You look great!" His glance met Barry Wilhelm's over Rachel's shoulder and he extended his hand. "Barry, you old son of a gun!" The two men shook hands and slapped each other heartily on the back. "Doesn't Rachel look fantastic?"

"Like a teenager," Barry agreed.

He introduced Ted to his wife, who fluttered her eyelashes and took Ted's hand in both of hers. "Ah'm delighted to finally meet the famous football star Barry has talked so much about. My goodness, you *are* big."

"I was hardly famous, Mrs. Wilhelm, and I haven't been on a football field in fifteen years." He took his hand from hers and patted his midsection. "The shape I'm in, I'd get killed if I tried it today."

She smiled up at him from beneath black lashes. "You look in fine shape to me, Ted." She even gave the name two syllables. "And don't you dare call me Mrs. Wilhelm again. I'm Adeline."

"Barry, how did you ever get this wonderful lady to marry you?"

"Beats me. Call me lucky," Barry said and Tess detected a tinge of irony in the words.

Adeline glanced sharply at her husband as Ted said, "Looks like we'll be surrounded by beautiful women all week." His glance took in Adeline, Rachel and, finally, Tess, who attempted to shatter the tense moment by drawing her guests's attention to the food.

"Please help yourself to refreshments," she said quickly. "What would you like to drink, Adeline? Coffee or tea?" For the next few minutes, Tess busied herself with serving the drinks. The four guests filled their dessert plates and found a place to sit, Barry and Adeline on the sofa, Ted and Rachel in wicker chairs angled toward the Wilhelms.

"I'm glad Franny suggested we all stay at the same place," Ted said. "By the way, where is Franny?" he asked Rachel.

"I haven't even seen her yet," Rachel said. "I tried her room, but there was no answer." She looked at Tess. "She has already checked in, hasn't she?"

Tess had poured herself a cup of coffee and was seated in a small plum-colored chair near the refreshment table, hoping to remain in the background while the three old friends caught up on each other's news.

She sat forward in the chair, her china cup cradled in both hands. "Ms. Alexander has been here since Wednesday. She didn't come down for breakfast today or you'd have seen her, Rachel."

"Wednesday! Why on earth did she come so early?" Ted asked.

"She's probably glad to get out of New York City for a while," Barry said.

"She says she's soaking up atmosphere," Tess told them. "For the book she's working on. She brought her laptop computer with her." Francine had also told Tess that she had wanted to get out of Manhattan so that her agent couldn't find her. Tess had the impression Francine wanted to fire her agent but was concerned about a contract she'd signed with the agency.

Tess had had her mind on a dozen other things when Francine was talking about her agent at breakfast one morning and couldn't recall the details. Francine tended to take over the breakfast table conversation if given the chance, which almost always happened as the other guests seemed to be intrigued with what writers did and wanted to ask them questions.

Frankly, Tess was a bit tired of hearing about the mysteries of Francine's creative imagination and her bouts with writer's block. Tess thought Francine took herself too seriously.

"How nice that she's working on a new book," Adeline remarked in a tone that implied the opposite. Definitely some jealousy there for her husband's high school sweetheart, Tess thought.

"She's had a long, dry spell," Adeline went on. "How long has it been since her last book came out?"

"Four years," Ted said quickly. He exchanged a look with Rachel who was sitting very straight and still in her chair.

Rachel cleared her throat and looked at Tess again.

"What does she mean, soaking up the atmosphere? What atmosphere?"

"I'm not sure," said Tess, who hadn't really thought much about it. Francine was always going on about vague things like atmosphere. But now that Rachel asked the question, Tess wondered what sort of atmosphere Francine was soaking up. To Tess, Victoria Springs seemed a fairly typical small town that happened to be invaded by tourists nine months out of the year.

"Hey," Barry said in an obvious effort to change the subject. "Guess who else is staying here. I caught a glimpse of him on the stairs earlier."

"Who?" Rachel and Ted spoke in unison.

"Albert Butterfield."

"Who's taking my name in vain?" inquired a silky voice from the doorway. Tess hadn't heard anyone on the stairs. Albert Butterfield must have tiptoed up them. Had he wanted to see if his old classmates were talking about him?

"Albert?" Rachel's voice rose in disbelief. "I didn't expect to see you. The last time I read your name in the newspaper, you were wheeling and dealing in Europe. I assumed you'd be too busy to come to a high school reunion."

"Hello, Rachel," Albert said coolly. Tess noticed he hadn't answered the question.

Barry Wilhelm looked at him with a touch of awe. Out of the corner of her eye, Tess saw Ted Ponte's eyes widen in surprise as they took in Albert Butterfield's clothes and self-assured manner. He stood and boomed good-naturedly, "It really is old Butterface, in the flesh! How're you doing, Butterfa—?"

"Don't *ever* call me that again." Albert hadn't raised his voice, but his steely look stopped Ted in his tracks.

Ted hesitated, looking embarrassed. Then, he pretended to think Albert was joking. He laughed and grabbed Albert's hand and pumped enthusiastically, oblivious to the cold hatred in Albert's pale blue eyes.

Albert Butterfield was smaller of stature than the other

two men, yet his mere presence was somehow substantial. There was a sense of control, of power being held in reserve. Though his sandy hair and long face were quite ordinary, his shrewd, assessing eyes drew others's attention like magnets picking up steel filings.

Barry Wilhelm was on his feet, too, and shaking Albert's hand. "We're honored you found the time to come to the reunion, Albert."

Albert's mouth crooked ironically. "I wouldn't have missed it, Barry. How's the campaign going?"

"Great. Super!" Barry said heartily, obviously pleased he'd asked. "I'd like you to meet my wife, Albert. Adeline, this is Albert Butterfield."

"Ah would have known you from your picture in *Forbes*, Mr. Butterfield," Adeline simpered, "although ah swe-ah it didn't do you justice."

Barely acknowledging the introduction with a nod, Albert sent a swift glance around the room. "Where's Francine?"

"Nobody's seen her," Ted said, "but I'm sure she'll be along. I don't guess Franny's changed much. She was always late for everything in high school."

Something about Francine's absence seemed to displease Albert. Like it or not, it appeared Tess was going to have to work at maintaining a congenial atmosphere with this group. "Mr. Butterfield," she put in quickly, "may I pour you some tea or coffee?"

"Coffee," said Albert crossly, looking toward the door.

Adeline rose gracefully from the sofa and laid a slim, manicured hand on his arm. "You just sit yourself down right he-ah, Albert. May I call you Albert? I'll fix your plate for you."

Rachel and Ted looked at Adeline, puzzled, while Barry beamed his approval. Adeline went to the table and picked up the silver serving ladle and a dessert plate. While Tess poured coffee, Adeline transferred a slice of lemon ginger pound cake to the plate.

"Somebody's coming," Ted announced. Unnecessarily,

as they could all hear steps clacking on the stairs.

Francine Alexander hurried breathlessly into the room and sang out, "Greetings all." Unlike Rachel, she hadn't kept her girlish figure. She was plump, to put it kindly, with arresting green eyes and a rosey complexion. But all of that was barely noticed because every eye went immediately to her dark red hair, which was thick and long and so shiny it dimmed everything else in the room. It fell in clouds of tangled disarray, as if she'd been out in a high wind. She wore jeans and a gauzy pink tunic. "Sorry I'm late." She exchanged hugs with Barry, Ted, and Rachel. She squealed, stepped back, and threw out her arms. "Are we the Four Musketeers, or what?"

Then, she seemed to notice Albert for the first time. She looked at him blankly for a moment before she realized who he was. "Well, look who's here," she cried and hugged him, too, much to Albert's obvious distaste.

As soon as Albert sat back down on the sofa, Adeline handed him a plate and coffee. He mumbled a barely audible thank you and Adeline's mouth tightened for an instant before she pasted on a determined smile and perched on a chair next to Albert's end of the sofa.

Francine, who still stood in the center of the room, looked down at her wrinkled tunic as though she'd never seen it before. An ink stain streaked across one breast. "Just look at me. I didn't have time to change. I've been writing. When my Muse is whispering in my ear, I must get it down while I can. Creative Juices are so capricious. They can stop flowing at any moment." When Francine talked about writing, she accented the esoteric parts as though they were capitalized.

Adeline's eyes raked Francine's broad beam as Francine went to the tea table. Then Adeline glanced at her husband with a self-satisfied smirk.

"I haven't had lunch or breakfast and I'm starving," Francine said.

She loaded her plate and carried it and a teacup to the couch and plopped down between Barry and Albert. Albert grimaced and scooted farther into his corner. Barry introduced Francine to his wife.

"Ah'm so pleased to meet you," Adeline said. "Barry has a picture of the two of you at your senior prom. I don't think I'd have recognized you, though."

"Really?"

"You were a smidgen thinner then." Adeline smiled brightly at her husband's old girlfriend.

Francine stiffened.

"Weren't we all?" Ted boomed.

Francine's green eyes barely touched Adeline before she turned back to her old friends. Between healthy bites of scone and cake, Francine began talking animatedly to Rachel, Barry and Ted.

No one but Tess noticed the venomous look Adeline gave her. Oh, dear, it was going to be a long hour. Suddenly, Tess wanted it to be over so she could run to the quilt shop for a rotary cutter and mat to use in cutting fabric strips for her quilt. Like most of the town's shops, it was open on Sunday afternoons during the tourist season.

"I called your room about an hour ago, Franny," Rachel said, "but you weren't there."

"I was walking. I'd been sitting at my computer since early this morning, and my body was threatening to lock in that position." She took a gulp of tea and went on. "I lose all track of time when my work's going well. The story just pours out as fast as I can type. It's almost a Mystical Experience."

Albert rolled his eyes and again, nobody noticed but Tess.

"When it's flowing, it's not always easy to turn it off, either. My characters were carrying on a conversation in my head all the time I was walking, so I came back and wrote it all down. Forgot about the tea until a minute ago. So I just jumped up and came as I was."

"You must be relieved to be writing again," Adeline purred, drawing Francine's eyes away from her former classmates. "After such a long time between books."

Francine's green eyes narrowed briefly. "I'm pleased you've followed my career so closely."

"Actually, Barry's the one who's done that. I haven't gotten around to reading your books yet."

Before Adeline could send another barb Francine's way, Tess rose quickly from her chair. "They're on the shelf behind you, Adeline," Tess inserted. "Perhaps you'll find time to read them while you're here."

"I doubt it," Adeline said flatly.

"Well . . ." said Francine. She seemed unsure how to take Adeline. "I know you must be busy with Barry's campaign and all." She gave Adeline a long, reflective look, as though she were wondering whether to put her in her place or ignore her. Then she gave a little shrug and turned her back on Adeline.

Nonetheless, Adeline seemed pleased by the exchange. Then she noticed that Albert had finished his cake. She jumped up and reached for his plate. "Finished already? Let me get you another piece."

"No, thank you," Albert snarled.

Tess could see that Adeline would try one's patience, but Albert sounded angrier than Adeline's fawning attention warranted. Tess wondered if he was feeling ignored by his classmates. She was sure Albert Butterfield wasn't accustomed to being ignored. She moved over to relieve him of the empty plate and refilled his coffee cup.

Cup in hand, Albert leaned back on the sofa and watched Francine with speculative eyes as she prattled on about her book.

"It's by far the best thing I've ever written. Sometimes when I'm writing I get goose bumps, it's so good."

"Lord preserve us," Albert muttered from his corner of the sofa. To which Tess added a silent Amen. If Francine heard Albert, she ignored him.

But Albert wasn't about to be ignored. "Another little love story, Francine?" he inquired. "What is it this time? Barbarians and slave girls? Sex-starved Apache chiefs and virginal white captives?"

Francine took a moment to force the corners of her mouth up before she turned and patted his knee. "I'm terribly flattered that you know what kind of books I've published, Albert. It means you must have taken the time from making all that money to read them."

"Not really," Albert said. "I just read the reviews."

According to Cinny, Francine's reviews of late had been scathing. Albert's clear dig must be humiliating to Francine and, indeed, her rosy complexion turned rosier. "I'm far more concerned with what my fans think, and they love my books. Critics can be so unkind. Of course, most of them are frustrated writers themselves, so they're jealous. It's amazing," she added, looking straight at Albert, "how many people cut down authors because secretly they wish they could get a book published."

Albert grinned wolfishly. "I'm sure you're right, Francine. It's the readers who count, and that comes down to sales, doesn't it? You writers like to talk about art and all that ethereal crap, but publishing is a business. The bottom line. That's all that matters in the end, and you're only as good as your last book. By the way, how *were* your sales on that last book? What did you call it? *Lust in the Dust*?"

Adeline giggled. She was obviously enjoying Francine's discomfort. Tess felt a surge of pity for Francine.

"*Love's Lusty Lady*," Francine snarled through clenched teeth.

Rachel inserted hastily, "Tell us more about your new book, Franny. Is it another romance?"

Francine stood abruptly, brushed past Albert, stomping on the toe of one shiny Italian loafer in the process. Albert muttered, "Cow," and jerked his foot back.

Having flounced to the tea table, Francine glanced over her shoulder and saw Albert rubbing the toe of his shoe with his fingers. "Oh, did I step on your toes, Albert? I'm terribly sorry." She neither looked nor sounded sorry.

"Bull," said Albert, still rubbing his toe. "You did it on purpose."

Francine laughed. "Don't be so touchy, Albert. And you

can stow the high-and-mighty act, too. You're not Mr. Big Business with us. We knew you when.''

"Well, know this," Albert snapped. "I could destroy you—" He whirled to stare at Barry. "And you—with a few phone calls."

Tess stared at Albert. Good heavens, where had all that anger come from?

Ted and Rachel exchanged an uneasy look. Francine had taken a combative stance, hands on hips. "Is that a threat?"

Albert's only response was a scorching glare.

Tess coughed to break the brittle silence and, to have something to do, began rearranging the silverware on the tea table.

Francine turned to the table to refill her plate, then went back to the sofa, sitting with her back squarely to Albert and Adeline.

Rachel cleared her throat. "About your book, Franny . . . ?"

Francine chewed slowly on a cookie before addressing herself to Rachel's question. Why did Tess get the feeling Francine had been giving herself time to frame her reply?

"The new book's a real departure for me, Rachel. Totally different from my other novels."

"Our hostess told us you've been here since Wednesday," Ted put in, clearly glad the conversation had veered away from Albert's threats. "Soaking up atmosphere, I believe she said. Don't tell me you're setting a book in Victoria Springs."

Francine gave him an enigmatic look and tossed her head to shake a mass of wild, brilliant red waves away from her face. "The town in my book is fictitious, Ted. I'm calling it Rose Meadows. I describe it as a small Missouri town, and I'm purposely vague about its exact location. But I'm a very visual writer. I need to have an image in my mind, as a pattern, so you may recognize a few familiar landmarks."

Barry glanced warily at the sulking Albert, then leaned forward to ask, "What's the book about?"

"I don't like to talk too much about a book while I'm writing it. It depletes my Creative Energy."

Albert's snort spoke volumes.

"All I can say is that it takes place in the '70s, and it has all the elements of a very big book. Love, passion, heartbreak, scandal, mystery, death . . ."

Barry shifted uncomfortably. "Now you've really piqued our curiosity. You can't stop there, Franny."

Francine smiled coyly. "The only other thing I can tell you is that it's about a group of high school friends. You know, the football captain, the student-body president, the beauty queen, the editor of the school newspaper." She paused, thinking, and the corners of her mouth angled up in a secret smile. She added, "The brainy class nerd." To Tess it seemed that Francine was throwing down a gauntlet. And Albert was just the person to take it up. The dislike between the two was palpable.

Eager to head off escalating hard feelings, Tess surreptitiously slid an empty silver tray to the edge of the table. It dropped to the floor with a loud thud. Rachel, Ted and the Wilhelms looked around, startled.

"Oops, sorry," Tess said as she scooped up the tray.

Albert and Francine were not diverted by her ploy, however. Albert was trying to shoot daggers through Francine's back with his eyes. Francine continued blithely, "You might say it's a coming-of-age novel."

She paused, waiting for their response. Nobody spoke. Francine looked uncertain, and finally she took in the electric tension that had gripped the room. "What is wrong with you guys?"

Barry broke the silence. "It sounds, well—kind of familiar, Franny."

Francine took a deep breath and placed a hand over her heart as though it pained her. "Oh, don't be so silly. All the characters are fictitious. That's what a novel is, you know. Fiction."

Her words did not relax the tension one iota. Tess scanned the faces of Francine's audience. It was a scene like no other she could recall at her genteel teas, one she would long remember.

Adeline's expression had turned from sulky to alert but perplexed. Ponderingly, she examined the faces around her, reminding Tess of a cat who'd suddenly lost sight of the mouse she was stalking and couldn't guess where it had gone.

Albert's long face was a stone mask, except for the swollen pulse beating in his forehead. Tess suspected if his blood pressure had been taken at that moment, any doctor worth his salt would have slapped him in the hospital immediately.

Barry's face was like a chalkboard over which an eraser had made a wide swath. He was almost as pale as the wicker arm of the sofa, and he seemed to be trying to communicate silently with Ted, who wouldn't meet his eyes. He shifted and cleared his throat, but Ted still did not look at him.

An odd sort of stillness had settled over Ted, except for his brown eyes, which were dark and brooding. Eyelids lowered, his gaze slid across the room, lit momentarily on the open doorway, then dropped and settled on the floral-patterned rug.

Rachel's beautiful face had crumpled, and there was an unhealthy pink in her cheeks. Something about the way she sat, staring fixedly at the slender hands clutched tightly in her lap, reminded Tess of a lost child.

Chapter 6

Somehow the atmosphere in the library never quite regained its initial congenial tenor. The old classmates talked about their families, their jobs, and the places where they lived, but the animation had left the conversation and, even with Tess's inserted leading questions, they couldn't seem to get it back.

Ignoring the others, Adeline worked valiantly at engaging Albert in a side conversation but seemed uncertain when he suddenly asked about her children.

"Laura just turned thirteen," she said. "Ah do de-*clare*. Ah can hardly believe it! Only yesterday she was a baby. Even though Laura has always been such a model child, ah almost dread her teenage years. Some of our friends have gone through fire with their teenagers."

"Really?"

"Oh, Laura is very well-adjusted, a good student, popular at school, so we don't expect any major problems with her."

"How fortunate for you."

"Ah have a picture of her in my purse. Ah'll show it to you later, if you'd like."

Albert's expression turned from amused to appalled. He must be wondering what he'd gotten himself into, thought Tess, repressing a smile.

Adeline went on, undaunted. "Everybody says she

looks exactly like me. When I put a picture of me as a teenager next to Laura's, we look like twins."

"You don't say."

Adeline seemed unsure how to take such a noncommital response, so she smiled and fluttered her eyelashes.

Albert leaned toward her and said in a confidential tone, "Don't you have a son, too?"

She studied his lantern-jawed face carefully before she answered. "That's right. Bobby's fifteen." Tess noticed that her hands suddenly gripped each other tightly in her lap.

"You don't seem eager to talk about him," Albert observed.

"That's ridiculous," Adeline sputtered. "Bobby's a dahlin. And so brilliant that we couldn't find a proper school for him at home. He attends a top-rated prep school in Switzerland."

"A prep school?" Albert's eyes were actually dancing. *What's he up to now?* Tess worried. *If he looked at me like that*, she thought, *I'd run for the nearest exit.*

Albert leaned back and crossed his legs. "A shame you couldn't find a school good enough for darling Bobby in this country?" he said silkily.

Adeline shifted in her chair. "Well, of course, we *could* have. I wouldn't want you to think we're snobs."

"Or the voters, either," Albert observed.

Adeline coughed delicately into her hand. "Er, yes."

Albert merely stared at her expectantly.

Tess glanced at her watch. Three forty-five. Would four o'clock never come?

"We thought it would be good for Bobby to experience another culture, just for a while," Adeline went on. "It was a very difficult decision to make."

"I see. Not many parents could bring themselves to send their child so far away. I'd think you'd miss him."

Adeline sniffed at the implied criticism. "Of course we do. Terribly. But we have to put Bobby's best interests ahead of our own."

His foot jiggled restlessly. "How unselfish of you," he said, suddenly losing interest. He turned away from Adeline and coughed loudly, interrupting the general conversation. He seemed angry again. Albert was clearly not getting the attention from his former classmates that he'd expected, except for Barry, who did try to include him by turning to him with a question now and then. Albert answered all of them with monosyllables. Like a contrary child, he wanted to be included but he sulked when anyone tried to draw him in.

At ten minutes of four, Albert excused himself and Tess breathed a sigh of relief. But Barry rose and followed Albert to the stairs. "If you have no plans for this evening, Albert, Adeline and I would like to take you to dinner."

"Sorry," Albert said shortly, "but I have business to conduct. I'll probably be on the phone for hours." He cast a significant look in Francine's direction. She grinned at him and tossed her red hair.

"Perhaps we could go out for a drink later then," Barry said.

"I'll call you if I get the time."

Barry returned to the library, his shoulders sagging. He looked at Adeline, who shrugged helplessly.

"Why do you want to spend time with that pompous ass?" Ted asked, which was exactly what Tess was wondering.

"Just trying to be sociable," Barry muttered. "And, for God's sake, Francine, why did you have to insult him?"

"He was asking for it."

"And you, Ted," Barry went on. "Why did you bring up that silly nickname?"

"Well, *excuse* me, but it slipped out." Ted laughed. "Old Albert did overreact a bit, didn't he? Still has no sense of humor."

"That may be why he wouldn't accept my invitation to dinner," Barry mused. "He was still mad about the way you two treated him."

"Forget Albert. I've got a much better idea," Ted said.

"Why don't the rest of us go to Harry's Grill for burgers and fries?"

Francine squealed and clapped her hands. "What a wonderful idea! I've already eaten at Harry's twice since I got here. Oh, the memories just flood over me whenever I enter the place, and I get this giant lump in my throat. You all know what a sentimental fool I always was."

"A fool, for sure," Adeline mumbled.

Tess began gathering up used cups and plates. Francine carried on, ignoring Adeline. "Harry's looks the same as it did when we were in high school. The burgers are just as good as they were then, too. And those curly fries . . ." She smacked her lips. "Good Lord, we practically lived at Harry's when we weren't in school."

"Yeah," Ted murmured nostalgically. "We made Harry's the *in* place."

"Incredible how all the other kids followed our lead on everything," Francine said smugly.

"I think I'll skip dinner," Adeline said, louder this time. "I feel one of my sick headaches coming on."

Barry stared at her for a moment and finally said, "I'll take a rain check, too."

Francine's face fell. "You were never a party pooper in the old days, Barry."

Barry avoided looking at his wife. "I'm a few years older now."

Francine shook her head sadly. "Looks like it'll be just three of us, then."

"Count me out," Rachel said. "Mom's fixing dinner for me at her place." She looked at her watch and jumped up. "Speaking of that, I'm going to be late if I don't get a move on."

Adeline and Barry followed her out. Adeline looked murderous, Barry merely resigned.

"Well, Franny," Ted said, clearly disappointed at the thinning of the ranks, "can I buy you a burger at Harry's?"

"Give me an hour to shower and get dressed. I'll meet

you in the foyer.'' Francine took his arm companionably as they left the library.

Tess watched them until they disappeared down the stairs and wondered what was going on in the minds of her guests. In spite of Albert's flare of temper and Adeline's jealousy, the others had, at first, seemed to enjoy being together again. But after listening to Francine go on about her book, they suddenly seemed eager to get away from each other. Possibly they were thinking Francine had turned into a colossal bore. Since it was his idea, Ted Ponte had been too polite to opt out of dinner, too, though Tess had gotten the distinct impression he'd wanted to when he learned Rachel wouldn't be joining them. Now Ted would have to listen to Francine through dinner.

With a perplexed shake of her head, Tess began setting plates and cups on a tray. If she hurried, she could still get to the Quilter's Nook before it closed at 5:30.

As Tess walked down the second-floor hall, carrying the loaded tray, Albert Butterfield stepped out of the Carnaby Room right in front of her.

"Miss Darcy—"

Tess jumped back, rattling cups and plates. He'd scared her half to death, popping out of his room like that. She took a deep breath. "Call me Tess, please. How may I help you?"

"I phoned City Hall, but it's closed. I'd forgotten it was Sunday."

Tess nodded, wondering what this had to do with her. She shifted the heavy tray in her arms. A gentleman would have offered to take the tray downstairs for her, but she'd already decided that Albert Butterfield was no gentleman. He was what Luke, a financial adviser, called a barracuda, somebody who got rich by feeding off the misfortunes of others. Albert had snapped up his high-tech company at a bargain-basement price when the former owner faced bankruptcy. A hostile takeover, Luke had said, whatever that meant. When Tess thought about it, she imagined Albert storming into the former owner's office and throwing him out. But she was sure that wasn't what Luke had had in mind.

However he had gained control, over the next few years Albert had turned the small, flagging company into a wildly profitable conglomerate. It was good business, Tess supposed, but she wouldn't want to make her living from other people's heartbreaks.

"You needed to speak to someone at City Hall?" Tess prompted. Her arms were beginning to ache from the weight of the tray.

"The mayor," Albert said. "Maybe you can tell me his name and I can reach him at home."

"*Her* name is Maribelle Yancy." Tess was quite fond of Maribelle, who had gone out of her way to welcome Tess to town and to invite her to several social functions.

Albert seemed taken aback. "A woman?" Tess wasn't surprised to learn that he wasn't just a barracuda, he was a sexist barracuda.

"Yes, and she's very good at the job." Tess felt compelled to speak up for the first female mayor of Victoria Springs.

"I'm sure," Albert muttered.

Tess couldn't let his sneer go unchallenged. "Maribelle succeeded in getting a sales tax passed to make improvements at the local hospital—after the two previous mayors, both men, had tried and failed. She isn't resting on her laurels, either. Now, she's working on getting a new combination gym and auditorium for the high school. Nobody would vote for another sales tax now, so she's organized a campaign for people to pledge money over a three-year period."

Albert looked interested. "Is that so? How much money is she trying to raise?"

"A million dollars." It sounded like an impossible amount when she said it aloud.

"And how much has been pledged?"

Tess sighed. "A little over a hundred thousand."

"Doesn't sound like the campaign has taken off like a rocket."

"Well, no," Tess admitted, "but Maribelle won't give up."

"If you'll excuse me, I have some business to conduct with Ms. Yancy."

"You won't get her," Tess said hastily as the door closed. It swung open again.

"Why not?"

"Maribelle's at a mayor's conference in Seattle," Tess explained. "She won't be back until next week."

He ran a hand over his thin, sandy hair, looking as though he suspected the mayor had left town merely to frustrate him. "Who's acting mayor in her absence?"

"Nobody, really."

Albert groaned. "I keep forgetting I'm in Victoria Springs."

Tess was sure he meant that as an insult. "Maribelle has organized the mayor's office so well that things run fine when she has to be away for a short period."

Now he looked angry, like a spoiled child who's been told he can't have dessert if he doesn't eat his dinner. "A veritable paragon, your Maribelle."

"Absolutely," Tess said curtly. She was usually more gracious to guests, but Albert Butterfield seemed to bring out the worst in her.

"But, surely there's a person designated to step in if needed. What if they wanted to give somebody a plaque or something?"

A plaque? Good grief. "If necessary, the chairman of the chamber of commerce board takes over for Maribelle on ceremonial occasions."

"And who would that be?"

Tess hesitated. She hated to sic this arrogant, self-important rooster on Luke, particularly on a Sunday. He was probably stretched out in his recliner watching a golf tournament. But, it wouldn't be hard for Albert to find out from another source. "Luke Fredrik," she said grudgingly.

Albert nodded. "Would that be Erik Fredrik's boy?"

"Yes. Luke's father passed away several years ago."

"Oh. I'm surprised. Erik Fredrik was the kind of man you expected to live to a ripe old age. Energetic. Walked everywhere. A hardheaded businessman, too. One of the few in Victoria Springs."

"Luke is a successful investment portfolio manager now," Tess said, wondering why she felt she had to keep building up her friends to this man.

"Hmmm. I didn't know that." He nodded again and shut the door in her face.

Chapter 7

Seated in the comfortable rose-colored armchair in the Carnaby Room, pad and pen in hand, Albert organized his thoughts before he made a single phone call.

Calls to make, he wrote. He paused to reflect upon the most efficient order. Albert was a very efficient and orderly man. He bent his head and wrote again.

> *Call Glenda at home.*
> *Instructions:*
> 1. *Find out where Bobby Wilhelm is staying in Switzerland. Get phone number and name of person in charge.*
> 2. *Contact Francine Alexander's publisher. Do they have a proposal for new book Francine is writing? Get a copy!*

Since the publisher had been a college fraternity brother of Albert's he was sure an appeal through the old boy network would get what he wanted. In fact, he did not consider any of these requests unreasonable. Not for Glenda, who frequently said she was as much private detective as secretary. He paid her very well, so he felt no compunction about calling her at home. She would grouse a bit, but he'd ignore that, as always. Since she was naturally nosy, she enjoyed

the little detecting jobs he assigned her from time to time.
It put a spark in her otherwise drab life.

He added a final note to Glenda's instructions.

Get back to me as soon as possible.
No later than noon Monday.

After more thought, he wrote,

*Write script for Glenda to use to contact editors of
newspapers in Kansas City, St. Louis, and Jefferson City—anonymously!*

Just in case. He would take care of the *Victoria Springs
Gazette* himself, since they would want to interview him,
anyway—after he made the arrangements for that little surprise announcement at tomorrow night's dinner-dance.

Let the four musketeers try to put him down then! Barry
and Adeline would turn green when they heard the news.
They'd think he was flaunting his success in their faces,
which he would deny, if they had the nerve to say it. Even
if it was the truth.

During the interview for the local weekly, he would clev-
erly drop a hint about the other story he wanted them to
pursue. The reporter would think it was his idea, of course,
probably be all lathered up over getting an exclusive. He—
or she—couldn't be too bright, stuck in a dead-end job in
a dead-end town like this.

Albert chuckled to himself. He was so damned good at
this behind-the-scenes manipulation.

He made a final note.

Call Luke Fredrik.

That tow-headed kid he remembered was now an investment adviser. Imagine that.

He spent several minutes writing Glenda's script for the

calls to the newspapers. Then, laying down the pad, Albert reached for the telephone.

A half hour later, Tess was carrying the last of the food left over from the tea down the second-floor hall when she heard voices coming from the Cliffs of Dover Room, the room she'd assigned to Francine Alexander. She would have thought nothing of it if she hadn't recognized the man's voice as Barry Wilhelm's. Where was Adeline, she wondered. Were Barry and Francine renewing their high school romance? But Barry's tone quickly disabused her of that notion.

"If you're telling the truth, you can easily prove it."

"I can't believe you'd accuse me of lying—*me*, Barry. After all we once were to each other."

"Oh, for God's sake. We aren't a couple of kids anymore, Franny. And stop that! You're only trying to distract me."

"Is it so easy?" Francine's voice had taken on a teasing note. "Adeline had better keep an eye on you. Tell me, when the two of you have sex, does she whisper naughty nothings in your ear in that exaggerated Southern belle drawl?"

"I said stop that."

"You've turned into a real bore, Barry. By the way, does dear Adeline know you're here?"

Tess took a step closer to hear Barry's answer. His laugh was bitter. "Do you take me for a fool?"

"I didn't think so."

"Don't change the subject. I want to see the evidence."

"Back off, Barry. I never let anyone see my work until it's finished." Francine wasn't teasing now. "It's still unformed. I don't want any judgments being made until I'm ready. I have to Shape my Material to my own private Vision. It has to be my Unique Voice the reader hears, without any outside influence. Do you understand?"

"Good Lord. I don't give a hoot about your unique

voice. When did you get so full of yourself, Franny?''

"An Artist must have faith in her Vision."

"I can see I'm getting nowhere. Look here, Franny. I'm in the middle of a political campaign."

"I know. You can't afford to have your precious reputation tarnished. Talk about being full of yourself. Well, trust me, you needn't worry about it. Now, if you'll excuse me, I have to change and fix my hair. I have a date for dinner."

"Incredible. Some things never change."

"What?"

"That always worked in the old days."

"What are you talking about?"

"You always used to get your way by saying you had a date with somebody else."

"Ah, you remember. How sweet."

"Wake up and smell the coffee, Franny. It's twenty years later, and I couldn't care less who you're sleeping with."

Francine muttered an oath. "I would love to stand here and listen to this cliché-ridden conversation all night, but I have things to do."

"We'd all be tarred with the same brush—including you. Have you thought about that?"

"More clichés," Francine clucked. "You need a new speechwriter, Barry dear. Well, I heard you the first time. Hadn't you better hurry back to Scarlett O'Hara before she comes looking for you?"

"By God, you're jealous!"

"Don't flatter yourself. Good-bye, Barry."

There was a long silence. Tess imagined the two of them standing their ground, trying to stare each other down. It would be interesting to know who looked away first.

By the time Barry stealthily left the Cliffs of Dover Room Tess had remembered her quilt shop errand and was halfway down the stairs, out of his range of vision. That's why she failed to see the tiny crack in Albert Butterfield's door and the two shrewd eyes that followed Barry from Francine's room to his own.

But Albert was in Tess's worried thoughts, nonetheless. That man was up to no good. She was sure of it. She wished she knew exactly what he wanted to talk to the mayor about. She'd gotten the impression that, whatever it was, Albert wasn't willing to wait. He'd contact Luke, and Luke would tell her all about it.

Adeline Wilhelm was so angry she could barely contain herself. Barry had left the suite while she was in the shower. He'd tapped on the stall door and yelled, "I'm going for a short walk." Before she could ask him to wait five minutes so that she could go with him, he had disappeared.

She grabbed a towel, ran to the suite door and peeked out. Barry never went for a walk, so she was understandably suspicious. And rightly so. She watched her sneak of a husband go into Francine Alexander's room. Right under her nose!

Several outraged impulses sped through her overheated mind—follow him to Francine's room, phone Francine's room and ask to speak to Barry, lock the suite door and refuse to let him back in. She discarded them all as unworthy of a Savannah Van Brunt.

Could Barry actually still find that woman attractive? What were they doing in Francine's room?

No, she wouldn't think about it now.

After drying off, she dressed and sat at the dressing table in the bedroom of the suite, which was separated from the sitting room by a beautiful Chinese folding screen, coral and blue lilies hand-painted on black lacquered panels. Behind her reflection in the mirror, the maple bed was clearly visible with its fabric canopy of bright coral roses on an ivory background. Coral to match the Darcy Flame iris which, according to Tess Darcy, had been bred by her late aunt, the former owner of Iris House before Tess inherited it and turned it into a bed and breakfast. Barry had said that Tess's grandfather, apparently an important man in the town in his day, had built it.

Adeline certainly approved of what Tess had done to the house. The suite she and Barry occupied was as nice as anything in Jefferson City. She decided to concentrate on that instead of what Barry and Francine were doing at this very moment.

That was easier decided than done. Turning her head to one side, she examined her still-perfect profile, firm chin and smooth neck. She worked out regularly at a spa and watched what she ate. She weighed within a couple of pounds of her weight when she married. No man in his right mind would prefer Francine Alexander to her.

So what was Barry doing in Francine's room?

On the other hand, did she really want to know?

She'd wager Francine was the instigator of their little tête-à-tête. She'd told Barry something to make him come to her room. But when? Adeline had been with Barry all afternoon and they had left the library together. Perhaps Francine had managed to slip him a note when her back was turned.

"Bitch." Adeline's hoarse whisper was full of venom.

She'd make Francine pay—and Barry, too. Van Brunts didn't get mad, they got even.

She heard familiar footsteps in the hall. Barry's. Adeline uncapped a metal tube and began applying lip gloss. By concentrating, she forced the hatred from her face and replaced it with a mask of supreme indifference.

Chapter 8

Francine stomped to the dresser and grabbed a hair brush. She began pulling it through her thick, red hair to get the tangles out before she showered. How she had looked forward to the reunion, but it was turning out to be downright depressing. What had happened to her fun-loving old friends? To think they had sworn a solemn oath, one dark, March night, to always keep each other's secrets and to come running if any one of them ever needed help. After seeing them again, she had the feeling that should she call them for help their response would be, *Francine who?*

The Cliffs of Dover Room was reflected in the mirror. She had been surprised and delighted to find such accommodations in Victoria Springs. Tess Darcy had spared no expense in remodeling the old Victorian house. The place inspired Francine.

In her room, walls, carpeting, love seat, gauzy-lace side curtains and quilted and lace-trimmed bed coverings were all creamy white, like the tall, bearded iris in the painting on the wall. In dramatic contrast, the bed and bedside lamp were of sculptured brass, and the skirted armchair and several throw pillows were covered with crisp, red-and-white patterned glazed chinz. A white ironstone pitcher on the intricately carved white dresser overflowed with red silk carnations. It seemed to Francine that the room had been created with her in mind. The creamy backdrop was the perfect one to set off her most flattering feature, her red hair.

Working on a particularly knotted tangle with the brush, she turned and looked over her shoulder to view her back side. She had been telling herself she might have gained a few pounds since high school, but she still looked fine. That was before she saw Rachel who, if possible, looked even better than she had when they were teenagers. In contrast, Francine didn't appear to have taken very good care of herself.

Writing was such sedentary work. Damn, her butt was getting as broad as an ax handle. Frankly, she had gained more than a few pounds since high school, more like thirty. She turned to food when she was tense, and the last few years had been full of stress.

But that was the past. She was on the right track with the new book, and she had to get the weight off before the book came out and the publisher sent her on tour. She'd start a diet and join a health club as soon as she got back to New York.

And have her hair styled. By the time the book hit the book stores, she'd be a knockout.

Her publisher had treated her so shabbily since the disappointing performance of her third book, that she might let somebody else have the new novel. It would be justified revenge, and she had no doubt that every publisher in New York would be crazy for it. Her new agent would surely decide to auction the book when she—or he—read the proposal. Francine hadn't yet settled on who that agent would be, having outgrown Rita De'Lane. What she needed now was one of the big names, somebody with power and influence in the publishing world. The right agent could start a feeding frenzy that could push the up-front money to over a million.

Francine closed her eyes and imagined it, sitting by her phone, taking calls from her agent as each new publisher upped the ante. *"It's at seven-fifty now plus a sixty thou bonus for the film option against six figures when the option is exercised."* *"Eight hundred thousand."* *"Nine-fifty."* *"A million!"* Francine licked her lips with delicious anticipation. It would be wonderful to be back on top again. And she'd make sure her old classmates, especially Albert Butterfield, heard about the deal. She was still furious over the way the little twerp had spoken so condescendingly to her. But she'd show him.

Francine couldn't wait.

It was five-fifteen when Tess rushed into the Quilter's Nook, causing the bell attached to the door to jangle loudly. The owner, Sandra Patterson, a fiftyish woman with round cheeks and a sweet smile, thrust her head around the doorway of the back room.

"Oh, it's you, Tess. I was just thinking of calling you. Everybody else in the beginning quilting class has picked up their supplies. I thought you might have forgotten."

"I've been very busy," Tess said breathlessly. "I'll just take the rotary cutter and mat today. There isn't time to look at fabric. Maybe I can get back tomorrow afternoon."

"I'm in no hurry to leave," Sandra said. "I'll just lock the door and we can choose your fabric without interruption. For the log cabin quilt, you'll need four fabrics in the same color from medium to light tones, and four in another color, medium to dark. Have you decided what colors you want to use?"

"Jade and rose, I think," Tess said. "To match my guest bedroom."

"Hmmm," Sandra mused. "That'll be a good contrast." She went to the door of the shop, locked it, and pulled down the shade. "Now, let's see what we can find."

Rachel didn't know what she could do to smooth things over with her mother except move out of her room at Iris House and back to the apartment. And she wouldn't do that. She knew that Coralee would relent eventually, but Rachel

wanted it to happen before she returned home. As much
for Coralee's peace of mind as her own. Grudges, long held
and nurtured, were debilitating. She ought to know.

Rachel took a second helping of chicken and dumplings,
which she didn't really want. "Mom, this is delicious. Nobody can make dumplings like yours. Believe me, I've
tried. They turn out either as tough as shoe leather or so
gummy they stick to your teeth."

Coralee Leander glanced briefly at her beautiful, older
daughter before she pressed her lips together and reached
for a hot sourdough roll. Coralee had once told Rachel that
she didn't know where Rachel came from, maybe she'd
been switched in the hospital nursery. She hadn't really
meant it, but Rachel understood why she'd said it. Her sister, Jane, was going to look very much like Coralee when
she got older; Rachel never would.

Coralee was short, stocky, and completely gray. She
wore her hair cut blunt and straight with bangs across the
front, as she'd worn it as long as Rachel could remember.
When she shampooed her hair, she brushed it smooth while
it was still wet, and that took care of that for another week.
She'd always said she couldn't be bothered fussing with
those things. Rachel had to admit, not caring what you
looked like made life simpler.

Coralee made no concessions to age, either. She looked
closer to sixty-five than the sixty she actually was. She'd
been nearly forty when she'd had to go out and get a job
for the first time in her life, and the only thing available to
a frightened, self-effacing middle-aged woman with no office skills was a night janitorial job at a local bank. For two
years, she had somehow managed to support herself and
her daughters with that job and had been fully resigned to
cleaning the bank for the rest of her working life.

Eventually, somebody had talked her into joining a sin-
gles support group, and with the encouragement of other
group members, she'd enrolled in secretarial courses during
the day. As Rachel was entering her junior year in college,
Coralee had been hired as a clerk at City Hall, where she

still worked. Rachel had been as grateful for her mother's day job as Coralee herself. Jane, who was eight years younger than Rachel, had needed her mother's presence when she came home from school. Rachel had worried so much about how Jane was handling things that she'd considered dropping out of college and coming back to Victoria Springs. Fortunately, Coralee's job at City Hall had made that unnecessary.

Since sitting down to dinner, Rachel and Jane had been carrying most of the conversation; Coralee was making it plain that she was still miffed at Rachel.

"The rolls are perfect, too," Rachel continued, determined to talk her mother out of her funk.

"If you like my cooking so much," Coralee bristled, "why are you staying at that expensive bed and breakfast?"

"Mom, I explained that," Rachel sighed. "If I were here, you'd wear yourself out cooking an elaborate dinner every evening."

Coralee sniffed. "I cook for me and Jane, anyway."

"Not like this." Rachel's glance swept the small kitchen table that was laden with rich food: chicken and dumplings, mashed potatoes and gravy, green beans almandine, carrot-and-cauliflower casserole, two kinds of salad—green vegetable and fruit—and homemade rolls. There was a fresh-baked lemon chess pie for dessert. Delicious, but the fat and cholesterol content must be off the charts. She hadn't eaten like this since she left home.

"She's right, Mom," Jane put in. "Don't be so hard on Rachel. We both have to work all day, anyhow. We'll see her about as much as if she were sleeping here."

"It's the principle," Coralee said. "What will people think, my own daughter not staying here. Like her mother and sister aren't good enough for her!"

Rachel's patience snapped. "You were always too concerned with what people thought," she flared. "Things might have been different if you hadn't been."

Rachel could feel Jane's surprised gaze on her, but she

was watching Coralee, who looked up sharply, a flash of pain in her eyes.

Instantly, Rachel regretted the burst of honesty. Unadorned truth was too hard for some people to hear. If it was the truth. Rachel wasn't sure anymore. "Mom, I'm sorry," she said, reaching out to touch her mother's hand. "I didn't mean that the way it sounded."

Coralee jerked her hand away.

Jane spoke up brightly. "I heard Francine Alexander's staying at Iris House, too." A plain, retiring young woman, Jane went through life defusing unpleasant situations. Her philosophy appeared to be: Deny anything too stressful or uncomfortable long enough and it will go away. It seemed to have worked for Jane, Rachel thought, meeting Jane's eyes and wondering if she'd ever really understood her sister.

As far as Rachel knew, Jane, at thirty, had never had, or wanted evidently, a serious romantic relationship. She was employed at the local library and still lived with their mother. Rachel wondered how much of her decision to stay in the apartment was due to Jane's inability to face the unpleasant task of telling Coralee she wanted to move out. But maybe she didn't want to. Jane seemed content with her lot in life.

"Francine's right across the hall from me," Rachel said in reply to Jane's words. "Barry and Ted are staying at Iris House, too."

Coralee frowned but Jane's expression remained merely inquisitive as she said, "Belva Hooker was in the library the other day."

"Making her rounds," Coralee muttered. "Picking up dirt."

Cinny had recently hired Belva as temporary help in the bookshop when Cinny's last employee had quit without notice. Cinny must have been desperate. Belva Hooker was the worst gossip in Victoria Springs.

Jane shrugged. "Well, you know Belva. Anyway, she says Francine's setting her new book in Victoria Springs and everybody in town is wondering if they'll be in it.''

Coralee gazed for a long moment at her younger daughter. She laid down her fork and pushed back her chair. ''Excuse me. I need to lie down. I'm not feeling very well.''

Rachel looked worriedly after her mother.

''It'll be okay,'' Jane said, unperturbed. ''Finish your dinner, Rachel. She's just trying to punish you. She'll get over it.''

Rachel stared at her and finally decided that Jane believed she spoke the truth. ''I'd better go and talk to her,'' Rachel said.

Across the street from the Queen Street Book Shop, Harry's Grill was packed with diners, and a dozen people were reading menus while standing up, waiting to be seated.

Ted Ponte sat at a corner table with Francine Alexander, drinking his third cup of coffee and wondering if Francine ever stopped talking. He wished she'd finish her cherry pie a la mode so that he could reasonably suggest they vacate their table in favor of some of the hungry-looking customers near the door.

In high school Francine had seemed never to have a thought in her head that was unrelated to clothes, dates, and having fun. Twenty years later and Ted couldn't guess how many pounds heavier, she rattled endlessly about things that Ted had never considered before, much less talked about. Like story reality and sequels and denouements.

And climaxes. Now, that was a subject he had often thought about, but he was pretty sure Francine wasn't referring to *that* kind of climax. He'd heard most of these words before, but not in the same context. It was like a code. Francine might as well be speaking a foreign language. Fortunately, she didn't require intelligent responses from him. This was a monologue, not a conversation.

As for what he had expected to find in Victoria Springs, that was something else again, something that had made him feel happy and eager when he'd thought about it in

Houston. On the whole, the feeling was so amorphous that, had Francine paused long enough for him to change the subject, he couldn't have described it.

It wasn't worth talking about, anyway. As soon as he began to experience the reality, the feeling had faded.

Francine was no longer a cute airhead; she was a crashing bore, a fat, crashing bore. Not that Ted had any room to feel superior in the weight department. Francine might actually be carrying fewer excess pounds than Ted himself. The difference was that his weight was distributed over six feet four inches of height. Francine was only five-six. He sucked in his stomach, feeling a little smug about turning down dessert even though his motive had had nothing to do with overeating. He'd wanted to get back to Iris House fast, away from Francine and into the blessed silence of his room.

That hope was dashed when Francine ordered dessert. Which she was managing to eat—slowly—without a noticeable break in the stream of words.

"The middle of the book," she was saying now, "can be ghastly. That's when the anxiety takes over and everything looks absolutely Black and Hopeless. You start to doubt the story premise, the credibility of the characters, your talent, everything."

"Mmmm," said Ted, which Francine evidently took as deep interest, for she went on in the same vein. Ted tuned her out.

He wondered if he should have skipped the reunion. Even his old best friend, Barry, had changed into somebody Ted hardly recognized. A politician. A phoney. And that wife of his!

Albert, on the other hand, was the same little snot he'd always been, only now he had the chutzpah to show it.

As for Rachel . . . Long ago he'd convinced himself that she couldn't be as exquisite as he remembered. That was before he'd walked into the Iris House library and felt as if the air had been knocked out of him. She was more beautiful than ever. But the darkness in her, which had been so well hidden in high school, was more pronounced. Or maybe it was only that he'd had twenty years to think about the reasons for it. Oddly it was Rachel, the one of the Four Musketeers who appeared to have changed the least, who had depressed him the most.

Ted was no stranger to depression. The doctor he'd seen in Houston had wanted to prescribe a mood-altering drug. Ted had refused. What good was it to mask your feelings when you went on being the same person?

A pill hadn't been made that could turn him into an overnight success. He had failed in pro football, he had failed in the sporting goods store, he had failed in marriage. He didn't even blame his ex-wife for leaving him, not much, anyway. She needed to find herself, she'd said, but what she'd really meant was that she needed to lose him. Initially, it had come as a shock; he'd had no inkling that she was so unhappy. But it had been some time since he had labored under the delusion that one person could ever really know another. And he'd quickly resigned himself to the breakup.

Even his fourteen-year-old son, Derek, had begun making excuses not to visit him weekends in Houston. He was lucky these days if he saw the boy every six months.

He wasn't setting any records in insurance sales, either. Which wasn't surprising, since he hated selling insurance. He just didn't know what else he could do.

He'd hoped the class reunion would give him the chance to enjoy the fantasy of going back in time. To be—just for a week—that green kid who'd been strong, tough and afraid of nothing, the football halfback who was idolized by the whole town. At seventeen he was on top of the world, and he'd thought everything was possible.

The problem was that everything wasn't possible.

Evidently meeting his old classmates again had added one disappointment too many to his overloaded psyche.

Now he couldn't feel anything—and that, he thought,

was a blessing. At some point his numb armor was going to crack and everything would cave in on him. Right now, he was numbly resigned, resignation being his chief coping mechanism. He'd been telling himself that things couldn't get worse.

The difficulty was that things could always get worse.

He knew how they could get worse, too; he just didn't want to think about it. But he realized, when he tuned Francine in again, that she wasn't going to let him *not* think about it.

"I haven't decided on a title, yet," Francine mused with a faraway look, as if she were thinking aloud. Which she probably was. Ted was convinced that, once she got going, every thought that entered her head immediately came out her mouth with no intervening filters. "Maybe you can help me with that, Ted."

He'd heard enough of her last thousand or so words to know she was still talking about the new book. He waited for her to go on.

"I want layers of meaning. You know what I'm saying? Something with the flavor of *The Good Old Days*. Only more profound, more subtle. That's my working title; though naturally, I can't use it on the finished book. It's too trite and obvious."

"How do you mean?"

"I mean that every adult knows the good old days weren't all that good. But when you're in high school, you haven't learned it yet."

"Unless you're old Butterface."

Francine laughed. "I'm talking about normal teenagers, Ted. Like us. We thought life would always be exciting and glorious, didn't we? We were the Four Musketeers. We led charmed lives. Nothing bad could ever happen to us."

She'd read his mind. Ted nodded glumly.

"During the course of the book, my characters will learn life isn't like that. By the end, they'll be forced by circumstances to face the grim, gritty reality that people are capable of the worst evils you can imagine and that life is filled with pain.''

Ted's heart was pounding. It was exactly what the four of them had learned. The more Francine talked, the more familiar the story sounded. The dimwit was actually going to do it.

''It's a dark book, the first one I've written that will end unhappily,'' she was saying. She actually wiped a tear off her cheek. ''Which will make the critics finally take me seriously. Literary novels always end unhappily.''

''What circumstances?'' Ted wedged the two tense words between bites of her desert.

She blinked at him. ''What?''

''You said the characters would be forced by circumstances to face real life. What circumstances?''

She scooped the last bite of cherry pie and melted vanilla ice cream, ate it, and blotted her lips with her napkin. ''I can't be specific, Ted, but—''

''Why can't you be?''

She cocked her head as if wondering how to explain Einstein's theory of relativity to a two-year-old. ''Because a novel is a Living Organism. It changes and grows as you write. The characters take over and run away with the story. Oh, it's such a rush when the characters get up and walk right off the page, take on a life of their own. You have to keep writing to find out what will happen next.''

Anger was seeping through Ted's numbness. ''Bull. You're the writer. You're in control.''

She laughed indulgently. ''I can see by your expression I'm wasting my breath. Nobody but another writer can possibly understand.''

''Cut the crap, Franny. The problem is that I understand too much. This afternoon you said everything in the book is fictitious. Then you admitted you're setting the book in Victoria Spring.''

''I did not—''

He overrode her. "You call it something else, but it's really Victoria Springs."

She shook her head. "No."

He leaned toward her. "You're lying. Admit it, Francine."

She hesitated, looking down at the soupy, pink streaks on her dessert plate as if wondering where the cherry pie and ice cream had disappeared to. For a moment, Ted thought in horror that she was going to order another serving. Finally, she looked up and sighed with strained patience. "There are a few similarities," she said finally. "Writers can't manufacture a novel out of thin air, Ted. A writer's imagination is limited by her experience."

"That's what I thought. Let's nail this down, ok? You're saying the characters and events are based on people you know and experiences you've had."

She heaved another deep sigh, as if wondering how he could be so dense. "Not in the way you and everyone else seem to think. All novelists's characters are composites of people they've known or heard about or read about. But transformed by the writer's imagination and shaped by the story requirements, the end result is unrecognizable."

Ted was beginning to feel again—with a vengeance, and what he was feeling was rage and panic. The woman could destroy them all with her poison pen. "Put another way, your career is on the skids, so you're stooping to shock and sensationalism."

She looked as if she'd been slapped. "I have no idea what you're talking about."

"Can the act, Franny. You know exactly what I mean."

She threw her wadded napkin on the table. "I don't have to sit here and listen to this!"

She had to be stopped. "We need to have a serious talk, Francine."

"Not now, Ted, not until you can be reasonable. I'm leaving. Are you coming?"

Ted dropped money for the check on the table and followed her from the restaurant.

Not only could things get worse, they could get intolerable. And would, if Francine couldn't be made to see sense. If she couldn't . . . well, he'd have to think of something else.

Chapter 9

Rachel reclined on a wicker chaise lounge in the Annabel Jane Room of Iris House, hugging a lacy white pillow to her breast, as she had clutched a teddy bear for comfort as a child. She hadn't changed from the mauve silk tunic and slacks she'd worn for dinner with her mother and sister.

Francine's room was directly across the hall. Rachel had knocked on the door when she returned to Iris House, but Francine wasn't there. She'd stretched out on the chaise to wait—and worry. The Sunday night TV movie would have been a welcome diversion, but she hadn't turned on the set for fear its sounds might cover those of Francine's return.

Ordinarily she would have found the room's lavender and green color scheme soothing. A framed watercolor of the ruffled lavender Iris for which the room was named hung over a delicately scrolled, white-and-brass iron bed. The chaise on which she lay was upholstered in lavender and spring green floral chintz, the same fabric used in the puffy, quilted coverlet. The wallpaper was striped in lavender and white, and the carpet was a calming gray with the barest hint of a lavender undertone. Antique lace adorned the bed's dust ruffle, the shade of the porcelain lamp on the bedside table, and numerous throw pillows. Wicker baskets overflowing with greenery filled two corners, another hung suspended on a brass hook over the lace-curtained window.

It was a graceful, lighthearted room, and until today Rachel had thought of it as a safe retreat. Unfortunately, even there she couldn't retreat from the thoughts swirling in her head.

When her mother had left the dinner table that evening, Rachel had followed her to the bedroom. She had found Coralee lying on her back with a damp washcloth over her eyes, the only light in the room coming from the adjoining hall. Seeing her mother like that had plunged Rachel, in a single instant, back to her childhood when Coralee had escaped reality by pleading a migraine and retreating to her room to take a sleeping pill and cover her eyes with a wet cloth.

According to Coralee, she hadn't taken sleeping pills in years; nevertheless, Rachel had looked around the room for a pill bottle. None was in evidence and when she spoke to her mother, Coralee's response had held no trace of the drugged slur the child Rachel had detested so much.

In hindsight, it seemed that Coralee had been in a drug-induced stupor every time Rachel had needed her. She knew that Coralee couldn't have been drugged out all the time, but memory is selective, particularly a child's memory.

She wondered sometimes what Jane's childhood memories were like. Jane never talked about it and Rachel had never asked.

Rachel had sat down on her mother's bed. "Mom, are you ok?"

Coralee had muttered something so soft as to be unintelligible.

"Jane and I will put the food away and wash the dishes. You just rest."

"I did the best I could," Coralee mumbled from behind the cloth. "I tried to be a good mother."

"I know," Rachel sighed.

"I hope when your daughters are grown they don't

blame you for every little disappointment they have.''

Little disappointment? Coralee's ability to sugarcoat facts was amazing. "Nobody's blaming you, Mom.''

Coralee had turned on her side, away from Rachel. "Yes you are; you always have. Go on back to your fancy bed and breakfast. Jane and I will be fine. We've learned to manage very well on our own.''

Did she really believe that? Rachel wondered. At sixty, Coralee might have lied to herself so long that she actually believed it, but could any young woman be truly content, living Jane's narrow life?

Perhaps so. On the surface, at least, Jane did not seem to harbor resentment or long for more than her job at the library and her mother's company away from work. But Rachel had the uneasy feeling that one day Jane's placid surface was going to shatter. She didn't even want to think about what might happen then.

Coralee had refused to say any more, so Rachel had left her to help Jane in the kitchen.

Standing beside her sister, who was rinsing dishes and handing them to Rachel to put in the dishwasher, Rachel had asked, "Does Mom still take sleeping pills?''

Jane had looked at her in bewilderment. "Still? I didn't know she ever did.''

Which told Rachel that Jane's memory was as selective as her own.

Jane had watched her place a plate in the dishwasher. "No, not there. We put the salad plates in front, the dinner plates in back.'' She had reached down and rearranged the plates. Rachel had noticed before that Jane was developing an old-maidish penchant for "a place for everything and everything in its place.'' If Rachel picked up so much as a magazine from the living room coffee table, Jane seemed to materialize at her elbow, when she was finished with it, to return it to the exact place it had been before.

Sad, dumpy, little Jane.

*   *   *

Hearing footsteps on the stairs, Rachel sat up quickly and laid the lacy throw pillow aside. She heard low voices, a man and a woman. It was only when the woman said, "Thanks for dinner, Ted," that she was sure it was Francine and Ted. Francine's words were followed by the sound of a door being opened and immediately closed again.

Then Ted said, "Francine?" There was no response. After a long moment, Rachel heard Ted's heavy footsteps going farther down the hall to the Black Swan Room.

She waited a couple of minutes before crossing the hall to knock on Francine's door.

"Go away, Ted!" Francine called.

Clearly Francine and Ted's dinner date hadn't ended well. "It's Rachel."

"Oh." After a long moment, Francine opened the door and peered out, her stance wary, her expression defensive. "Hi, Rachel."

Not exactly a gilt-edged invitation, but Rachel couldn't let that stop her. "Can I talk to you, Franny?"

Francine groaned and raked both hands through her flowing mop of red hair. "Another country about to be heard from, eh? Well, why not," she said in a resigned tone. She stepped back for Rachel to enter. "Everybody else has forced their uninformed opinions on me. Why should you be different? But make it fast, Rachel. I want to go to bed."

It was a night for star gazers—and lovers, just enough breeze to draw the June heat from the bricks of Tess's small, private terrace and tantalize the nostrils with the scent of new-mown grass. After Tess had returned from the Quilter's Nook with her quilt supplies and fabric, Luke had called to suggest they go out for pizza. Now they sat in a gently rocking glider, Tess's head resting on Luke's shoulder. The side door to Tess's apartment, the north half of the ground floor of Iris House, was ajar to allow the soft strains of Barbra Streisand's "The Way We Were" to reach them.

June weather was as nearly perfect as weather got in Missouri, and Tess couldn't think of a single way she would rather spend a balmy June evening than to share the glider with Luke and feel the weight of his arm around her shoulders and the warmth of his lips brushing her temple now and then.

Primrose, Tess's gray Persian, had even deigned to join them. She lay in Tess's lap, meticulously cleaning her front paws. Tess sighed with contentment and closed her eyes. After another tiring Sunday, she could so easily fall asleep right there. And she might have if Luke's voice hadn't stopped her.

"Are you unhappy, sweetheart?"

Her eyes flew open. "What have I to be unhappy about?"

"Nothing that I know of. It's the music. That's a very sad song."

"I suppose," Tess agreed.

"You must have had a reason for choosing it."

"I love Streisand, for one thing. And maybe having all those people here for their high school reunion has put me in a nostalgic mood." She turned her head to look at him.

"Who's staying here?"

She listed the names of her guests and added, "Quite an interesting little gathering we had at tea today. Do you remember any of them?"

"Hey, they're here for a twenty-year reunion. I'm not that old."

His mock-injured tone made her smile. "I know, dear. You're. what?—five years younger than they." And handsome and successful, to boot. But what Tess really loved about Luke was his ability to take things in stride. He managed the investment portfolios for about two dozen well-heeled clients from his home office, connected to Wall Street by computer, modem and fax machine. And he handled even that high-pressure occupation with equanimity.

"Six, at least," Luke corrected.

"Hmmm." Tess did a quick calulation. "So you were still in the elementary grades when they were in high school."

"A mere baby," Luke agreed.

"But Victoria Springs was even smaller then than it is now. You must remember something about them."

"Sure. Ted Ponte, the football halfback, was my hero—mine and every other boy my age. We were crushed when he fizzled out in the pros."

She reached up and placed her hand over the hand that rested on the curve of her shoulder. "Not as crushed as he was, I'll bet."

He linked his fingers through hers. "That's true, but it was my first lesson in real-life heroes. They're apt to have clay feet."

Yes, Tess mused. Attributing perfection to human beings was always a mistake. "What about the others? Do you remember anything about them?"

He pulled back a little so that he could focus on her face. "Why are you so interested?"

Tess shook her head. "I'm not sure. I just have the feeling something's going on with them, something that could be connected to their mutual past."

"After what happened in April, I thought you swore not to get involved in your guests's private lives."

He was referring to the murder of one of Tess's guests during the weekend of Iris House's grand opening. Frankly, if she hadn't done some snooping on her own, the police might never have solved that case.

"I just want to satisfy my curiosity, that's all. This isn't a murder investigation."

"Well, I'm sorry, love." Luke's curiosity clearly did not match her own. "In those days, I was too busy building clubhouses and playing ball with my friends to worry about what was happening at the high school—except for football, of course. I know a little about Francine Alexander and Albert Butterfield, but only because of what they've done since leaving Victoria Springs. The local paper has run articles on both of them. You know the kind: local boy and girl make good.''

Yet both Francine and Albert seemed to have an insatiable need for continued recognition. ''Speaking of Albert Butterfield, he wanted to contact the mayor about something. I told him Maribelle was out of town and gave him your name. Did he call you?''

There was a pause. ''Yes.''

His hesitation intrigued her. ''And?''

He took advantage of her upturned face to kiss her. Primrose protested the suddenly too-close quarters by growling and snapping her fluffy tail. Tess reached to scratch behind her ears as Luke broke the kiss and murmured, ''What were you saying, sweet?''

He was sounding far too innocent to be believed. She sat up, putting several safe inches between her mouth and his. Pleased with the added space, Primrose snuggled down and purred.

''I had the distinct impression that Albert Butterfield is up to something,'' Tess said.

His face was set in sober lines, but his eyes were smiling. He loved tweaking her curiosity. ''You're a suspicious soul, Tess.''

She wasn't going to be deterred. ''What did he want, Luke?''

''Oh,'' he said blandly, ''he extended his sympathy on the death of my father. Now, where were we?'' He placed a hand at the back of her head, pulled her to him and kissed her decisively.

Primrose, her limited patience at an end, howled, jumped off Tess's lap and stalked into the apartment.

Tess's patience was slipping, as well. She planted her hands on Luke's chest. ''Luke! Your father has been dead for five years. Albert Butterfield wouldn't have called you after all this time just for that. What are you keeping from me?''

"What a thing to say, dear heart." He reached out and traced the line of her cheek.

She caught his hand. "Don't try to divert me." She waited.

"Well, there is something I need to ask you. How would you like to attend a dinner-dance with me tomorrow night?"

He was looking at her with a gleam in his eyes. "All right. But the only dinner-dance scheduled for tomorrow that I know of is the one at the high school. It's part of the twenty-year reunion activities."

"Right. I've been invited and I can take a guest."

"You? Why would they invite you?"

"For my scintillating company?"

"Luke!"

He grinned and placed a finger on her lips. "Save your breath, Tess. I can't answer your question. It's a deep, dark secret—until tomorrow night."

Tess would have stamped her foot had she not been sitting down. What deep, dark secret could Albert Butterfield have shared with Luke? And how frustrating for Luke to refuse to share it with her. As if she couldn't be trusted to keep a secret; it was almost insulting.

But she knew Luke could not be badgered into telling what he didn't want to reveal.

Something was definitely afoot around here, though, and it wasn't just this mysterious secret shared by Albert Butterfield and Luke. From the way the old classmates staying in Iris House had reacted to Francine Alexander's upcoming book, they had some secrets of their own. Maybe Gertie could enlighten her. All of Gertie's fifty years had been spent right here in Victoria Springs. Tess would speak to her about it tomorrow morning. As for what Albert Butterfield was up to, it was plain she'd have to wait until tomorrow night's dinner-dance to be enlightened on that subject. It was probably some new acquisition he'd made or award he'd won that he wanted Luke to announce at the reunion so he could bask in the envy of his former class-mates. The man had an ego the size of St. Louis.

She sighed and settled back in Luke's arms. Tomorrow's questions couldn't be answered until tomorrow.

As for now, her mind was turning to other things, for Luke was kissing her again.

Chapter 10

Early Monday morning, Tess left her apartment, crossed the glazed tile floor of the Iris House foyer, passed through the guest parlor and dining room and entered the kitchen. Gertie, in a wine-and-blue floral tent dress with a white-bibbed apron tied around her ample waist, was arranging toasted English muffins in a large baking dish.

Gertie was in her element in a kitchen—any kitchen. She enjoyed eating good food as well as cooking it and had long ago given up on having what she called a "beanpole figure like those magazine models."

"I'm storing fat for a famine," she'd once told Tess wryly. Gertie had the ability to laugh at herself. She was a naturally positive person, which she attributed to the fact that she ate what she wanted and didn't worry about it. At the moment, she was humming contentedly to herself.

As for Tess, she was feeling less than positive this morning. She'd had a restless night; she kept waking up to puzzle over the deep, dark secret that would be revealed at that night's dinner-dance—the secret that Luke maddeningly refused to share with her.

All that her puzzling accomplished, however, was to keep her awake.

After viewing her tired brown eyes in her bathroom

mirror, she had spent a full five minutes on makeup, which she usually dashed on in less than thirty seconds. She was wearing a navy blue cotton shirtwaist dress with a white collar and cuffs to complete the picture of the well-rested proprietor of Iris House ready to tackle another busy week.

Tess was somewhat restored by the smell of freshly brewed coffee and the mere sight of the familiar, big, airy kitchen with its pressed tin ceiling, lace curtains and brick-colored tile floor. She liked the room so much that she had the contractor build a scaled-down version of it in her apartment next door.

Tess helped herself to coffee from the pot. "Good morning, Gertie."

Gertie set the pan of English muffins on the kitchen's center work island. "'Morning, Tess. Looks like another beautiful day." She bent to adjust the oven thermostat.

"Hmmm, yes." Tess sat down at the round oak table. "Eggs Benedict this morning?" Gertie was generally acknowledged to be the best cook in Victoria Springs, and Tess loved everything she prepared. But Gertie's carefully guarded recipe for eggs Benedict was exceptional, even for her, a creation fit for the gods. When asked to reveal her secret, she'd shrug and say, "Oh, I just add a couple of extra spices."

"Uh-huh," Gertie said in answer to Tess's question. "With kiwi fruit and some outstanding fresh raspberries I found at the farmer's market. I saved a bowl of them for you in the refrigerator."

Tess jumped up to get the bowl and took it to the table. The raspberries were indeed beautiful—big and dark red and practically bursting with juice. Tess sprinkled on a teaspoon of sugar, then spooned a berry and popped it into her mouth. "Oh, these are lovely," she murmured.

"Told you so. I took a gallon of 'em home to freeze. I'll bring you a raspberry pie. Maybe Luke can be persuaded to help you eat it."

Persuaded? "Oh, that'll be a tough assignment," Tess

teased. "You know how much Luke loves your pies, Gertie."

Gertie's eyes lit up at the compliment. She thought Luke was the best catch in town and Tess suspected she also thought that Tess didn't fully appreciate him.

"I can't do anything else till the first guests come down," Gertie said. Going to the glass-fronted white cabinets, she took down a stack of plates and set them on the center island. Then she poured herself a cup of coffee and joined Tess, looking unusually pleased with herself.

"Ok, what gives?"

"Huh?"

"You're bursting to tell me something."

"How did you know?"

"You look like Primrose when she's caught one of those blue jays who love tormenting her," Tess said. "Come on, what is it?"

Gertie laughed. "I won two hundred dollars at bingo last night."

"Well, congratulations. What are you going to do with it?"

Gertie thought about it. "Guess I'll buy that spice rack at The Antique Gallery for my kitchen. I should have enough left to get a used portable typewriter, too."

Tess looked up in surprise. "A typewriter?"

Gertie shrugged modestly. "I've been thinking about putting together a cookbook of my recipes. All the new ones I see in the book stores are low fat or no fat or low cholesterol. If you ask me, the time's right for a return to good, old-fashioned food."

Tess grinned. "You may be right, Gertie."

Gertie rested a plump arm on the table and peered more closely at Tess. "You're not looking too pert, girl. Did you have a short night?"

So much for Tess's carefully applied camouflage. "A restless one."

"You worried about something?"

Tess ate another raspberry, savoring the sweet-tart taste. "Not worried, exactly. Curious."

"Ah." Gertie's gingery eyebrows rose quizzically. "You know what curiosity did to the cat."

Tess brushed that aside with a wave of her hand and ate another raspberry.

Gertie went on. "You got a house full of new guests yesterday. Does your curiosity have anything to do with them?"

Tess admitted that it did. How well Gertie knew her. Tess named the guests and tried to describe the undercurrents she had sensed during the Sunday tea in the library, but it was difficult to put her feelings into words.

"Well," Gertie said when Tess gave up trying, "they're not the only ones interested in Francine's new book. Everybody in town's talking about it. Afraid she'll paint Victoria Springs in a poor light, I expect, now that she's living in New York City."

Tess pursed her lips in reflection. "This was more than concern over how the town will be depicted. Francine's book is set in the '70s when she was in high school here. The other guests—except for Adeline Wilhelm, of course— seem to think Francine is putting *them* in the book."

"I take it they aren't flattered."

"Absolutely not. They're worried."

"Why?"

"That's one of the questions that kept me awake last night."

Gertie shook her head. "More likely they're feeling self-conscious. Besides, most people have a few things in their past they wouldn't want printed in a book for the whole world to read."

"I suppose."

"Take poor Rachel Waller. I doubt she wants to be reminded of that time."

Tess frowned. From Rachel's reaction to Francine's new book yesterday at tea, Gertie was right. But Tess couldn't imagine what might have happened in Rachel's youth that could be so upsetting. "From what I've heard, Rachel was the most popular girl in high school," she said. "You'd think she'd enjoy being reminded of those days."

Gertie leaned closer to Tess. "She had a lot of friends, sure, but it's her home life I'm referring to. Ralph Leander, Rachel and Jane's father, was one of those domineering males. Ran his house like a boot camp with him as the drill sergeant."

"Really?"

Gertie nodded gravely. "And that's not all. He used to go on drinking binges. Wasn't above hitting them. Coralee and those girls were afraid to say 'boo' when he was drinking."

Tess sipped her coffee thoughtfully. "I can understand why Rachel wouldn't want her family life exposed. But why would Francine want to put that in her book?"

"We've both heard how Francine goes on at breakfast," Gertie said with a scowl. "She probably means to paint everything bigger than life. I expect writers have to exaggerate to impress the readers. Anyway, that's what Francine would probably say."

A loud knock at the back door that opened off the kitchen made them both jump. "Nedra," Tess said as she got up to open the door.

"Sounds like she's trying to break the door down," Gertie said with a chuckle. "That woman goes at everything full tilt."

Nedra Yates, Tess's housekeeper, was a tall, lanky woman without an ounce of visible fat on her. Originally, Tess had hesitated before hiring her. Nedra looked so fragile. But Gertie had given her a good recommendation and Tess would be forever grateful that she had. Nedra could outwork a lumberjack and have enough energy left to go home, fix dinner for her mechanic husband, and accompany him to the Elks Lodge for an evening of bingo.

Nedra wore her usual work attire—faded jeans and a cotton shirt. "Have a cup of coffee, Nedra," Tess said. "Nobody's down for breakfast yet."

"Might as well take all that weight off your feet," Gertie said, only half good-naturedly. More than once, Gertie had pointed out how unfair it was that Nedra could eat like a horse and never gain a pound, while everything Gertie ate went to fat.

Nedra laughed and brought a steaming mug to the table. She plunked down in a chair and looked inquiringly at Tess. "Reckon you already heard about Gertie's big win."

"Indeed I have."

Nedra's fine, straw-colored hair was slicked back and held in a clasp at the nape of her neck. By the time she finished cleaning Iris House that afternoon, however, half of it would have escaped confinement to form a wild halo around her angular face. Nedra's hair was untamable, but she kept trying.

Nedra clutched her coffee cup with both bony hands and took a cautious sip. "Downright lucky," she muttered. "Me, I ain't never won more'n fifty dollars on bingo." She sighed, took another swallow of coffee, and changed the subject abruptly. "Full house, Tess?"

"Almost," Tess said. "The last guest won't arrive until after noon. She'll be in the Arctic Fancy Room, so you can skip it today."

"Tess and I were just discussing the others," Gertie said.

"Class reunion bunch," observed Nedra, who tended to speak in sentence fragments. Her mouth often seemed unable to keep up with her mind, which caused her to start speaking mid-thought.

Fortunately, Tess and Gertie were adept at filling in the blanks of Nedra's spotty conversation.

"You remember that little twerp Albert Butterfield, Nedra?" Gertie asked.

"Yep. Nose bloodied two, three times a week."

"Lawd, yes," Gertie exclaimed. "I'd almost forgotten how the other kids used to pick on him."

"Came bawling to her at the Hair Affair," Nedra said.

"Nadine Butterfield, you mean. That's Albert's mama,"

Gertie clarified for Tess's benefit. "She was a beauty operator. Retired now."

"Surprised he'd show his face," Nedra said.

"Why, he's rich now," Gertie reminded her. "Probably came to thumb his nose at the rest of 'em. Is that his big Lincoln parked out front, Tess?"

"Yes, but it's rented," Tess said. "He informed me that he owns three Mercedes but he couldn't spare the time to drive from home."

Nedra whistled appreciatively. Gertie batted her eyes and exclaimed, "Three! That's what I call overkill."

Tess finished her fruit, then fetched the coffeepot to refill their cups. She sat back down and turned to Gertie. "Now, what were you saying about the Leanders?"

Nedra snorted. "Not worth the powder it'd take to blow his brains out."

"Rachel and Jane's father?" Tess asked and Nedra looked at her as though she thought Tess needed a hearing aid. "Gertie was saying, before you came, that he had a drinking problem," Tess added.

"Hummph," Nedra muttered. "More like a stopping problem. Real mean drunk."

"That's what I was telling Tess," Gertie said. "According to Olivia Perkins, Coralee and the girls used to hide out at her house when he got real bad."

Nedra frowned. "Who's Olivia Perkins?"

"She's close to ninety years old. Lives at the nursing home. I visit with her every month when I go out there with the missionary society. Olivia and her husband—he's been dead for years—used to live across the street from the Leanders."

"A blessing when he left," Nedra snapped.

"Ralph Leander, you mean?" Tess asked, wanting to be sure she had the facts straight.

"That's what I said."

"He deserted Coralee and them two girls, Tess," Gertie explained. "Rachel was still in high school and Jane was

just a little thing. He'd been drunk for two days, the way
I heard it. Got mad about something.'' Her lip curled in
disgust. ''Probably didn't think his dinner was cooked just
right or his shirt wasn't ironed to his satisfaction. Olivia
saw him driving away about midnight. Said his tires was
squealing and he was zigzagging down the street, bouncing
off one curb and then the other. A wonder they didn't find
him dead and his car wrapped around a telephone pole. But
they didn't. He just drove off and never came back.''

''Blessing,'' Nedra pronounced again.

''In some ways, I guess it was,'' Gertie agreed. ''But in
other ways, no. I don't reckon they had much money in the
bank and, from what I heard, he never sent them any. Coralee couldn't keep up the payments on the house. The mortgage company took it back and they moved into the
apartment where Coralee and Jane still live.'' She shook
her head sadly. ''Coralee was downright pitiful.''

''Like a whipped pup,'' Nedra inserted.

Gertie nodded in agreement. ''Scared of her own
shadow. Had to go out and get a job for the first time in
her life. Before that, she only left the house when she had
to. *He* wanted her at home, I suppose.''

''Did she try to find him?'' Tess asked.

''Huh,'' Gertie responded. ''What for? She musta been
glad to see the back of him.''

The selfishness of Ralph Leander's desertion made Tess
indignant. Imagine not even caring if your own children
had food on the table. ''She should have taken him to court,
made him pay child support.''

''I expect she was afraid to,'' Gertie said. ''Afraid he'd
come back and hurt her or those girls.''

''Sleeping dogs,'' Nedra mumbled.

Let them lie, Tess finished silently and automatically.
That was one way of looking at it, Tess supposed. But
Ralph Leander had gotten away scot-free and left his family
to suffer the consequences. No wonder Rachel sometimes
had the look of a lost child. Both she and her sister must
have permanent emotional scars from their childhood.

No one would want to be reminded of a childhood like that, much less see it published in a book. Couldn't Francine see that? Writers were said to be sensitive, after all. And wasn't Francine Alexander supposed to be Rachel's friend?

Then, surely, she wouldn't . . .

But Francine was awfully self-absorbed.

Maybe Tess could find out for herself what was in that book Francine was working on. Francine's old friends might be wrong about the book's subject matter. If Tess could satisfy herself of that, she could report to Rachel that her fears were unfounded.

Maybe when Francine was out she could . . .

She brought herself up short, shocked by what she was considering. She would never snoop through a guest's personal belongings.

No, there had to be another way. Maybe she could invite Francine to her apartment for coffee. She'd get her talking about the book. *That* shouldn't be difficult. Francine did love to hear herself talk about her work. If Francine talked long enough, Tess could probably learn whether Rachel needed to be worried.

The phone in Albert Butterfield's room rang promptly at 8 A.M. Glenda was nothing if not prompt.

"Got most of what you wanted, Mr. B.," the secretary greeted him.

"What do you mean *most*?"

"I got zip from Francine Alexander's publisher. Nada. Zilch."

"Ok, ok," Albert said impatiently. "I get your drift. The question is, why."

"Evidently, she hasn't turned in a proposal in over a year. They have no idea what she's working on now. To tell the truth, they aren't all that interested."

Hugging her dirty, little secrets close, Albert thought furiously. But if he couldn't outsmart Francine Alexander, he didn't deserve half the business success he'd had. He had to find out what was in that book, one way or another.

"About Bobby Wilhelm," Glenda went on. "He's at a place called The Alpine School."

"Sounds like a ski school," Albert muttered.

"Hardly. Once I had the name, I called a friend of mine who teaches in the most exclusive private prep school in Chicago. Here's what she said about The Alpine School."

As she went on, a big grin split Albert's face. This was even better than he'd hoped. "You contact those papers immediately with an anonymous tip," he said. "You took down what I told you to say?"

"Every word, Mr. B."

"Ok." He'd make sure the local rag got the story for Thursday's paper, which was the only day it came out.

"Anything else you need?"

"Not at the moment." Albert started to hang up, then snatched the receiver back to say, "You're a good secretary, Glenda."

"Good? Why, I'm outstanding."

Getting Francine alone to invite her for coffee, turned out to be a problem for Tess. Francine left Iris House immediately after breakfast and still hadn't returned by late afternoon when the guest for whom the Arctic Fancy Room was reserved arrived. At that point, the sight of her new resident knocked all other considerations right out of Tess's head.

When Tess answered the doorbell, a bizarre female shouldered past her into the foyer and dropped a suitcase that must have weighed a ton on the glazed tile floor. For starters, she had a crew cut and three dangling gold earrings in one ear. The other ear was bare. Green eye shadow had been applied to her upper lids with a heavy hand clutching, it appeared, a trowel; and her black mascara was as thick as library paste. She was dressed in a flowing tunic that was almost as long as her ankle-length green skirt. Hanging from the orange and black tunic were fringes and beads and what looked like scarves in various bright, clashing colors.

But most amazing of all were her boots. They appeared to be combat boots. Tess looked twice to be sure. They *were* combat boots.

"Oh, Gawd." The woman sank down on her suitcase. "I thought I'd never find this town." She glared up at Tess with snapping, black eyes and said accusingly, "I flew from New York this morning—after a two-hour wait in the plane on the runway. Then I spent a horrific afternoon driving all over the damned southwestern quarter of Missouri."

"I'm sorry," Tess said and barely managed to stop herself asking why the woman hadn't found a service station and asked for directions, or at least a road map.

She seemed disinclined to accept Tess's apology. "Tell me why people would set a town down out here in the middle of nowhere. Hills and trees all over the place. Keeps you from seeing more than a few yards ahead of you."

"Well, uh—" Tess supposed there weren't many hills or trees in New York City. She could think of no appropriate answer, so she offered her hand. "I'm Tess Darcy, proprietor of Iris House."

Irritably, she waved Tess's hand away. "Rita De'Lane. I have a reservation."

"Yes, of course, Ms. De'Lane. We have the Arctic Fancy Room ready for you."

She squinted at Tess. "The Arctic which?" With all that mascara, it was a miracle her lashes didn't stick together and blind her.

"Arctic Fancy."

"What the hell is that supposed to mean?"

"All of our rooms are named for irises." Iris House was named for Tess's Aunt Iris, who'd been an iris grower and breeder. The rooms were named for some of the beautiful species of irises surrounding the house.

Rita De'Lane sat there with her jaw dropped for a moment. "Irises. You mean like the flower?"

"That's right."

"Iris House. I get it. But damned if I believe it."

Tess bristled. She'd put her heart and soul into making

the bed and breakfast a success. And she was already in the black. There had been a waiting list of potential guests ever since her opening day. She couldn't stand hearing her pride and joy belittled. First, Mr. Big Bucks Butterfield had appeared totally unimpressed by her beautiful bed and breakfast and now this nightmarish vision of a woman had the nerve to—

Tess took a deep breath and counted to ten. "It's quite true."

"It probably is," she muttered. "I saw a shop in town called Knick Knack Knook. All *K*s." She pushed herself to her feet with a weary groan. "Well, lead the way. You can have the porter bring my suitcase up."

Porter? Where did this freakish female think she was, the Hyatt? "I'm afraid we don't have a porter," Tess said.

Rita De'Lane gaped at her. "Surely you don't expect *me* to carry it up those stairs. Hey, lady, I'm frazzled. There's no way I'm hauling that thing another step."

Tess counted to ten again. She had an idea she might be doing that quite a lot while Rita De'Lane was around. "I'll bring it." She grabbed the handle in both hands and hoisted the suitcase. She struggled up the stairs with the suitcase banging against her legs. What on earth did the woman have in there, more combat boots?

When she saw her room, Rita De'Lane looked around and said grudgingly, "It's—nice. A pleasant surprise. Frankly I was ready to settle for anything with indoor plumbing."

Tess bit her tongue and forced a smile to her lips. "I'm ever so pleased that you approve."

"By the way," Rita said as Tess started to leave. "Where is Francine Alexander staying?"

"You know Francine?"

"We're great friends. I wasn't sure until Saturday that I'd be able to join her. I'd like to surprise her."

Somehow there was a false ring to her words. But it wasn't exactly a state secret where Francine was staying.

"Francine's right next door to you. The Cliffs of Dover Room."

"Cliffs of Dover. Unbelievable. Well, see ya later." She ushered Tess unceremoniously from the room before Tess had a chance to say that Francine was out.

Tess walked back downstairs, fuming. Rita De'Lane was incredibly rude. *Middle of nowhere, huh? Pleasant surprise, indeed.* How dare she ridicule Victoria Springs and Iris House, a woman who went out in public looking as if she'd picked up her wardrobe from trash dumpsters!

And she claimed to be a friend of Francine's. In fact, she'd said they were *great* friends. Tess's opinion of Francine went down another notch. Breakfast tomorrow should be interesting with Rita De'Lane added to the mix.

Tess made up her mind to ignore the De'Lane woman. If she continued to insult Victoria Springs, Tess would do as her father would have advised, consider the source. She let herself into her apartment, thinking about what she would wear to the dinner-dance. Tess preferred being comfortable to looking like a fashion plate, so her entire wardrobe of party clothes consisted of two outfits. The wine velvet skirt and fitted jacket would smother her in June. That left the pencil-slim, floor-length black crepe skirt with the white silk shell top.

The black skirt and silk shell would have to do.

Primrose was in the sitting room, napping in her favorite chair, which featured a Renaissance revival design with a medallion on top and a comfortably padded seat. She looked up as Tess entered and yawned and stretched lazily. Then she sharpened her claws a few times on the cushion.

Tess sighed. She had bought a scratching post designed for cats to sharpen their claws on. But Primrose ignored it. The cat had staked out that chair as her personal property, and Tess was resigned to having the cushion recovered periodically.

"Hello, sweetie," Tess greeted the Persian. She stroked Primrose's thick, silky, gray fur. Primrose began to purr as her eyes drifted closed. "You are such a spoiled girl," Tess said, scratching behind Primrose's ears, "but a gorgeous one."

Primrose meowed and purred louder in agreement. When Tess stopped scratching, she opened one yellow eye to look at her accusingly.

"Sorry, your highness, but I have things to do." There was just enough time to press her outfit, shower, and dress before Luke arrived.

Primrose jumped off the chair and followed Tess to the kitchen, where she wound in and out between her legs a few times.

After giving her one final stroke, Tess hummed a light-hearted tune as she got out the steam iron. Primrose sat down in the middle of the kitchen, her fluffy tail curled around her legs, and watched Tess intently.

"You know I'm going out tonight, don't you?" Tess asked the cat, who had begun washing her paws. "I must give off some kind of vibes."

Tess found the kitty treat box in the pantry and gave Primrose two of the crunchy morsels.

Primrose was mollified, for the time being.

Tess got the ironing board from the kitchen storage closet and pressed the black skirt and silk top. She'd wear her pearl necklace and ear studs with it.

Even though it wasn't her high school reunion and she probably wouldn't know any of the guests except for Luke and the people who were staying at Iris House, she was actually looking forward to the evening.

Before it was over, her curiosity about what Albert Butterfield had confided to Luke would be satisfied. Whatever that was, she was sure of one thing. It would draw attention to Albert Butterfield, the attention he seemed to crave from his former classmates.

After what Gertie and Nedra had said about Albert's childhood in Victoria Springs, Tess was more inclined to forgive his seeming egomania. At least, she now understood why he acted as he did.

At any rate, it should be an eventful evening.

Chapter 11

Luke took Tess's hand as they cut across the school ground, giving it a squeeze.

"Did I tell you you look particularly lovely tonight?" he asked.

"Only once," Tess told him, "but I think I can stand to hear it again."

His teeth flashed white as he smiled down at her in the moonlight. He looked quite dashing himself in a black tux with a tucked white shirt and red satin cummerbund, his blond hair silvered by the moonlight.

"I didn't expect you to wear your tux. I didn't realize this was such a snazzy affair."

"I imagine we'll see everything from the most casual clothes to the height of evening fashion," Luke said. "I wore this because I'm making an important announcement."

"I know," Tess said with a sigh. "Don't rub it in." He still refused to tell her what was going on.

He chuckled. "All will be revealed in due time, love."

Tess knew better than to try again to worm it out of him. He accused her of being obstinate when she got her teeth into something, but he could be downright stubborn himself.

They skirted one end of the rectangular high school building.

"This is where they're going to build the new auditorium and gym," Luke said. "It was always in the plans, so they left plenty of room for it when they put up the original building. Once the construction is complete, they'll convert the present gym into an all-purpose room for meetings and such."

"Now, if only they had the money to add on."

"Have patience, Tess," he counseled.

Patience wasn't Tess's long suit. "I'll try, but I don't think Maribelle's pledge campaign is going very well. Too soon after the sales tax vote, I guess."

"You never know. Sometimes these things just take off, for one reason or another."

That was vintage Luke, with his laid-back attitude toward life. Everything will work out all right, he often told her—because, of course, everything always did for him.

In the moonlight the plain buff brick high school glistened palely. A very ordinary structure by day, it looked enchanted tonight. And why not? There was a certain magic about class reunions. They transported people back in time.

Golden light shone in the tall windows and spilled from the large glass double doors marking the entry.

Tess felt a little tingle of anticipation. Luke was going to make an "important announcement," but beyond that, she hadn't been to a dance in ages. The only time she'd ever danced with Luke was on the tiny, crowded dance floor of a local roadhouse. After carefully maneuvering among the crush of perspiring bodies through two tunes, they'd given up and gone home.

As they approached the school, one of the large glass doors swung open and an attractive, blond woman in a green satin dress and dyed-to-match high heels greeted them.

"Welcome! I'm Martha Gunn—used to be Martha Mahoney."

Luke introduced Tess and then, himself.

"I remember you, Luke," Martha said.

"Are you any relation to the Dick Mahoney who owns the local Texaco station?" Tess asked.

"That's my dad." She looked closely at Tess. "Surely you're too young to have been in my class. And as I recall, Luke, you were several years behind me, as well."

"That's right, and Tess is new in town. We're here at Albert Butterfield's invitation."

"Oh." Briefly, Martha looked bewildered. She gestured toward the long table in the foyer, which was tended by two women in sequined evening dresses. "Albert's already here somewhere. He's the only other man I've seen wearing a tux. Make yourself name tags before you look for him. Otherwise, everybody will be racking their brains, wondering why they can't remember you from our class."

Tess and Luke were pinning their name tags in place when Francine Alexander descended on them in a swirl of white chiffon. Her bright red hair was pulled back on one side and held in place with a sequined comb.

"What are you doing here, Tess?" Her green eyes took in Luke and her expression shifted from mild curiosity to deep interest.

"You'll have to ask Luke," Tess said, suppressing a smile. "Luke, this is one of my house guests, Francine Alexander."

"Luke Fredrik," Luke said, accepting Francine's plump hand. "I'm representing the Chamber of Commerce. And you, of course, are the famous author."

"How sweet of you," Francine purred. "And how lovely of the Chamber to send you. There's a photographer from the newspaper here, too. I didn't know class reunions aroused so much interest."

Tess caught a flicker of amusement in Luke's blue eyes. A newspaper photographer? That had to be in connection with Luke's "important announcement."

"That's a pretty dress, Francine," Tess said. The only problem was that the design had been meant for a younger and slimmer woman. The white chiffon had a full, floor-length skirt and a low neckline that displayed Francine's generous cleavage. "You must have come back to Iris House and changed while I was getting ready."

"No. I took my clothes with me when I left this morning. Changed in the rest room at the library."

"The library?"

"I spent the entire day there, doing research. Mostly reading old newspapers. Had a splitting headache from looking at the microfilm screen all day. The things we Artists do for our Art."

"I hope your headache's gone now," Tess said.

"A couple of aspirin took care of it. I'm fine."

If Francine hadn't been back to Iris House, she probably didn't know her friend Rita De'Lane had arrived. Before Tess could mention it, though, a short, dark woman in a red sheath dress rushed over on spike-heeled shoes and grabbed Francine's arm.

"Francine Alexander!"

Francine looked at her blankly for an instant before recognition dawned. "Peaches? Peaches Martin?"

"Oh, Lord," Peaches squealed, "I haven't heard that old nickname in twenty years. Franny, I'm so proud of you. I have all your books. I just *love* them. Especially *Passion's Purple Blooms*. I've read it five times."

Francine glowed. "Why, thank you, Peaches."

Peaches pulled on Francine's arm. "Come with me, Franny. I want you to meet my husband. He's never really believed I went to school with a famous author."

Francine wiggled her fingers at Luke and Tess as she was dragged away. Her public called.

Tess would have to catch Francine later and tell her that her friend had arrived.

Starting across the room, Tess spotted Rachel Waller and Ted Ponte. Rachel, in a simple yellow silk street-length dress, looked breathtaking. Ted wore a navy business suit with a bright-colored tie. They had their heads together, talking quietly. Fanning the old embers? Tess wondered, but then she drew close enough to hear Ted say, ". . . researching old newspapers'' and got a good look at their faces. Ted's expression was grave and what was going on with Rachel? She looked as though she'd been crying.

"Let's find Butterfield," Luke said as he led the way through the rest of the milling crowd in the foyer. "I thought I saw him over in that corner. Yes, there he is."

"I've already got a table staked out," Albert said when they had exchanged greetings. "The photographer is holding seats for us. Let's go on in."

The gymnasium had been transformed. Blue and silver crepe-paper streamers (evidently the class colors) were draped from the center of the ceiling to the walls, where they fell almost to the floor, all the way around the room, creating the effect of an elaborate tent. Centerpieces of blue and silver carnations decorated tables that were spread with blue cloths. The lights were dim, adding an air of mystery and romance.

Five band members were setting up their instruments at one end of the gym. The tables would have to be pushed together at the other end to make room for dancing after dinner.

There were places for six at each table, and people were beginning to drift into the gym now. Albert led Tess and Luke to a table near the speaker's stand. Only one chair at the table was occupied—by Rick Masters, a young man with tousled, mud-colored hair, the photographer for the *Victoria Springs Gazette*. His camera rested on the table in front of him.

Both Luke and Tess knew Rick casually. They exchanged hellos and sat down. Rick's nervous fingers fiddled with his camera, his napkin, his silverware, while he watched Albert alertly.

"When will this big announcement—whatever it is—be made, Mr. Butterfield?" Judging from his restlessness, he had been led to expect something momentous and could hardly wait.

"Right after dinner, before the dancing starts. I've already alerted the reunion chairman.'' He glanced at Luke. ''I told him you had a few words to say that I was sure everybody would want to hear.''

''You are a master of understatement,'' Luke said.

Albert looked pleased with himself.

''Is that all you told him?'' Luke asked.

Albert's thin lips curved in a satisfied little smile. ''I didn't want to lose the element of surprise.'' His gaze drifted past Luke and he stiffened. ''Oh, hell, they're heading this way.'' Tess glanced over her shoulder to see the Wilhelms approaching the table.

''Quick,'' Albert hissed, ''let's grab somebody—any-body—for those two empty seats.''

By this time, the Wilhelms were close enough to hear what Albert said. Barry's stride slowed for a moment, and then he squared his shoulders and came on.

Before anyone else could react, Barry and Adeline reached the table. ''Hello, everybody,'' Barry boomed with determined cheerfulness. ''May we join you?''

Everyone looked at Albert who had slumped back in his chair. He remained silent while looking churlish. A thor-oughly unpleasant man, Tess thought, but she wasn't about to cater to the rude millionaire. After all, the seats were unclaimed. ''Of course,'' she said and ignored Albert's dark scowl. She introduced them to Rick Masters, who rose to shake hands with Barry. After shaking Luke's hand, Barry stretched out his hand toward Albert, but Albert ig-nored it. Tess wanted to kick him.

Barry's hand fell to his side.

Rick Masters spoke into the embarrassed silence. ''I heard one of the reporters say he's doing an article on you for Thursday's paper, Representative Wilhelm.''

Albert shot the young man a black frown. Rick looked confused and glanced away.

Now, what did that mean? Tess asked herself, staring hard at Albert, who didn't seem to notice. Did he expect them to refuse to talk to the Wilhelms just because he appeared to have a problem with their sharing the table? *What an impossible boor!*

"I wonder why I haven't been contacted for an interview?" Barry asked.

"You probably will be," Rick murmured and risked another look at Albert, who stared back, as though daring Rick to say any more. *What on earth is going on with Albert?* Tess wondered. Did he resent Barry's getting his name in the paper?

Barry turned his dazzling smile on the young man and held Adeline's chair, the one next to Albert. He wore a conservative, but expensive, black suit. Adeline's gown was mint green with tiny seed pearls stitched in a rose design on the bodice.

"How are you, Albert?" Adeline inquired, patting his arm, which he pulled away rudely. Valiantly, Adeline pretended not to notice and produced a weak smile. "You've been out and around, haven't you? Ah haven't seen you since breakfast."

"I phoned your room all morning," Barry said. "We wanted to take you to lunch."

"I've been busy," Albert said curtly.

"What about tomorrow, then? Before Franny's autograph party."

"I'll be busy tomorrow, too."

"Then—"

Albert leaned his elbows on the table and looked squarely into Barry's face. "Let me spell it out for you, Wilhelm. I'm not going anywhere with you. I told you this morning that my accountant says I shouldn't make any more charitable contributions this year. Do I have to put it in writing?"

He had, in fact, told Barry as they were leaving the breakfast table, in the hearing of most of the other guests. Tess thought Albert could have chosen a more appropriate time and place. He apparently enjoyed humiliating Barry at every opportunity.

An embarrassed silence followed Albert's words. Then Barry said testily, "Can't I invite an old friend to lunch without wanting something?"

"We were never friends," Albert returned.

A flush rose in Barry's cheeks. Tess felt sorry for the poor man. She wondered why he kept trying to buddy up to Albert when all he got was the brush-off. Did he really need campaign money that badly?

Luke spoke into the crackling silence. "Speaking of Francine Alexander's autograph party, Tess, aren't you helping with that?"

Tess nodded and squeezed Luke's hand under the table, a silent thanks for jumping into the breach. "So is Aunt Dahlia. Cinny says she and one employee can't handle all the sales she expects to make and take care of the refreshments, too."

"Does she really expect to sell many of Francine's books?" Albert inquired of Tess in a disbelieving tone.

"Oh, yes. Cinny says local authors always sell well and, after all, Francine has been on the best-seller lists."

"A fluke," Albert muttered.

Tess bristled. "I haven't read Francine's books, but obviously a lot of people like them."

He shrugged off her words. "Let her have her puny fifteen minutes of fame."

Nobody seemed to know how to respond to that. Except Adeline, who giggled nervously. Fortunately, a woman appeared at their table at that moment to take drink orders.

A local women's club catered and served the dinner—a green salad followed by a tender filet mignon served with twice-baked potatoes, a fresh vegetable medley, and hot rolls. Dessert was apple cobbler.

Tess turned down dessert and excused herself to repair her lipstick in the ladies' room. Francine Alexander followed her from the gym and caught up with her in the hall.

"There's a rumor floating around that Luke Fredrik is going to make some big announcement tonight, Tess. That's why he's here, isn't it?"

"So he tells me."

Francine leaned toward Tess and asked in a confidential tone, "What's he going to say?"

"You know as much about it as I do, Francine."

Francine waved a hand. "Come on, Tess. I won't breathe a word to anybody. You can trust me."

"I really don't know, Francine."

Francine didn't seem to believe her. "Honestly?"

"Honestly. Luke wouldn't tell me."

Francine studied her. "Now I'm really intrigued."

No more than I, Tess thought. They had reached the rest room, and Tess put out her hand to push open the door. "By the way, Francine, a woman checked into Iris House this afternoon who says she—"

From the opposite end of the hall, a strident voice rang out—"Francine Alexander!"—it could probably be heard everywhere in the building, not to mention the next county.

Tess paused with her hand on the door. Francine, clearly recognizing the voice, gasped and whirled around. The voice belonged to Rita De'Lane, who ran toward them, her silver-studded, black cowboy boots clacking loudly on the tile floor of the hall. She was moving faster than Tess would have dreamed possible, given that she was wearing a short, black skirt that was so tight she must have greased herself to get into it. With the skirt, Rita wore—Tess blinked her eyes several times to make sure she wasn't seeing things. But her vision was just fine. Rita De'Lane had on what looked for all the world like a long-lined, white bra. Tess had seen Madonna in something similar in a music video. A bustier, she believed it was called. But no matter what you called it, it looked like underwear to Tess.

Rita came to a halt in front of them. The four black hoops dangling from one earlobe swung back and forth. She thrust her excessively made-up face in Francine's stunned one. "Francine, I have to talk to you."

Francine stumbled backward a step. "What are *you* doing here?" she sputtered.

Rita shook a black-nailed finger in Francine's face. "Muhammad wouldn't come to the mountain, so . . ." When she lifted her arm, Tess feared her breasts were going to pop out of the bustier. Amazingly, they didn't.

Francine took another step back and planted her hands on her round hips. Her face had taken on an unhealthy hue. "I can't believe this. You tracked me down. You've got a nerve!"

"Yes, I have."

"How did you find me?" Francine demanded.

Uh-oh. They didn't sound like great friends to Tess. She felt a beading of sweat on her brow. If the women came to blows, she didn't know what she would do.

Rita's eyes narrowed, bringing black mascara-laden lashes together. "I have my ways," she said.

Francine snorted.

"Actually, it wasn't very hard. You'd never make it as a secret agent, Francine." Rita slid a glance in Tess's direction. "In fact, I'm staying in the room next to yours at Iris House."

"*What!*" Francine glared at Tess. "How could you put her in the room next to mine?"

Tess threw her hands out helplessly. "She said you were friends and she wanted to surprise you."

"Friends, ha! She's my agent."

So, this was the woman Francine wanted to fire. Frankly, Tess could understand why. Did people actually dress like that in New York City?

Francine huffed angrily and pushed open the door to the rest room. She stalked inside. Tess followed. So did Rita De'Lane. Francine whirled around, her hands balled into fists. "This is a class reunion, Rita. You weren't invited."

"Pardon me while I cry my eyes out," Rita retorted sourly.

"Then leave!"

"Gladly. As soon as we reach an understanding."

"Are you insane, Rita? I came here to attend a class reunion, yes, but I also wanted to get away from New York.

I don't want to talk to you. That should be obvious by now, even to you."

"I gathered that when you didn't return my phone calls." Rita shrugged and, again, Tess waited for the woman's breasts to be completely exposed. It didn't happen.

"So you decided to stalk me?"

"Let's not get dramatic, Francine. We have business to discuss."

"I have nothing to say to you." She brushed past Rita. "Now, if you'll excuse me, I need to use the facilities." She went into a stall and closed the door.

"You can't stay in there all night, Francine," Rita yelled at the closed door. "You're going to have to talk to me. Sooner or later. I am your agent, Francine."

"Not for long," Francine yelled from behind the door.

Tess walked around Rita and slipped into the stall next to the one Francine occupied.

"I heard you've been looking around for other representation behind my back," Rita said shrilly. "There are no secrets in the publishing world, Francine. You ought to know that by now. Everything else aside, it's unethical to be interviewing agents without first informing your present representative of the fact."

"Oh, please. What do you know about ethics?"

The sound of flushing from Francine's stall drowned out Rita's reply. Then the door was flung back hard enough to bang on the metal partition separating Tess's stall from Francine's. Francine stomped out. "You want to be informed? Ok. You're fired, Rita."

"It's not that easy."

Francine made a sound of utter frustration. "Wrong. It is exactly that easy."

Rita muttered a string of oaths that scorched Tess's ears. If they dressed like Rita De'Lane in New York City, perhaps they talked like her, too. If so, Tess was grateful to be living in conservative, small-town middle-America.

Francine's exasperated breath could be heard clearly in Tess's stall. "Not that I owe you any explanation, Rita, but because of our past relationship, I'll try to penetrate that hard head of yours. I have reached a crossroads in my career. At this point, I need a power agent—''

"What you need at this point, Francine, is a miracle."

Francine raised her voice and went on. "—someone who can up my advance by merely walking into an editor's office. I'm afraid you don't fill the bill.''

"You silly bimbo!"

Francine gasped. "Why, you—''

Rita's shrill voice overroad Francine's. "Allow me to open your eyes to reality. You aren't the hot property you seem to think you are."

"Then why did you come all the way to Victoria Springs to talk me into staying with you?" Francine sneered.

Tess stood in the stall, hoping that one of them would leave any minute. She wanted to get back in time for Luke's announcement.

"Because I'm angry, damnit!" Rita was saying. "After all I've done for you—to be treated this way . . .''

"What have you done, Rita? You couldn't sell my last three proposals.''

"Nobody could have sold them. As for influence, if I hadn't had plenty, that awful third book of yours would never have sold, either.''

"Awful? You said it was a well-crafted novel.''

"I lied!''

"This is just sour grapes, Rita. You're fired, and you can't change my mind. So why don't you accept it and go on back where you came from.'' Francine uttered a harsh laugh. "You will be a laughingstock if you stay in Victoria Springs. People don't dress like that around here.''

"So I've noticed. That chiffon must be left over from the '50s.''

"Insulting me won't change my mind, Rita.''

Tess was beginning to feel ridiculous, hiding behind the metal door. Clearing her throat loudly, she came out of the stall and went to a basin to wash her hands. The other two women didn't seem to notice. Rita had maneuvered Francine into a corner, but Tess decided that Francine could take care of herself.

"You've forgotten one minor, little detail," Rita said. "You signed a contract with the agency. It's still in effect, and it will be for another two years. *Then* you can decide whether you stay or go. In the meantime . . ."

Francine pushed roughly past Rita. "In the meantime, hell! People break those contracts all the time. Our relationship is over, Rita. I'm leaving you and your agency."

"I don't think so."

"Oh, really? Just what do you think you can do to stop me?"

"Whatever it takes." Rita's tone carried a deadly determination that made Tess shiver.

The argument did not seem to have lost any steam, and Tess didn't want to hear any more of it. She skirted Rita and Francine, whose ample bulk partially blocked her way. "Excuse me, please. I have to get back."

"Wait, Tess!" Francine jostled Rita getting around her and caught up with Tess at the door. "I'll go with you."

"This isn't over, Francine," Rita yelled as the rest-room door swung closed in her face. "We'll talk tomorrow."

"Idiot!" Francine muttered. "Can you believe that woman?"

"She is rather flamboyant."

A tense laugh escaped Francine. "That's one word for it." Francine looked over her shoulder. "Thank goodness, I don't think she's going to follow me."

Tess was relieved to leave Francine at the gym door as they headed for their separate tables. When Tess was seated, however, she continued to watch the door, half-expecting Rita De'Lane to follow Francine inside and continue the argument. Clearly, Rita had a cast-iron nerve, and she didn't mind making a scene.

Luke leaned over to speak into Tess's ear. "I thought I heard shouting in the hall."

"You did. There was even more of it in the ladies' room."

"What's going on?"

"I'll explain later," Tess whispered, still watching the door. When, after several moments, Rita had not appeared, Tess relaxed and turned her attention to the podium as the emcee, a man she didn't know, walked up to it.

"Is everybody happy?" he asked the crowd who responded with a round of applause.

"Wasn't that a great meal?"

More applause.

"Before we clear the floor for dancing, there are a few announcements. First off, don't forget the book signing for Francine Alexander tomorrow afternoon at the Queen Street Book Shop. Franny will be there from two to four. Then, at five, we're all gathering at the city park for a picnic." He looked up from the piece of paper containing his notes toward Tess and Luke's table. "And now I want to ask Luke Fredrik, chairman of the board of the Victoria Springs Chamber of Commerce, to come to the podium for one final announcement."

Rick Masters grabbed his camera and followed Luke to the podium.

"On behalf of the Chamber," Luke said, as Rick Masters positioned himself facing the podium, "I'd like to welcome you all back to Victoria Springs. It may have changed a little in the last twenty years, but the people are the same friendly folks that you remember. Now—" Luke smiled at Tess. "Albert Butterfield, will you come up here, please."

Amid a murmer of curious whispers, Albert strutted to the podium, his expression one of utter self-satisfaction. *You'd think he'd just stolen another business from some poor, struggling person who'd worked hundred-hour weeks to make his dream reality*, Tess thought unkindly.

Luke put a hand on Albert's shoulder as he looked down at the much shorter man. Rick Master's flashbulb flashed.

"I got the surprise of my life Sunday evening when Mr. Butterfield called me," Luke said. "We had a long and gratifying conversation about Mr. Butterfield's desire to give something back to his old home town." Every eye in the room was trained expectantly on the two men. "It is my privilege tonight, ladies and gentlemen, to announce that Mr. Butterfield has made a contribution of one million dollars to build a new auditorium and gymnasium for the high school. It will be named the Albert Butterfield Wing." Another flashbulb went off as Luke shook Albert's hand. "I thank you, Mr. Butterfield. Victoria Springs thanks you." He stepped back so that Albert could speak into the microphone.

After a moment of stunned silence, gasps could be heard around the room. This time the applause was thunderous.

Tess happened to be watching the Wilhelms. All the blood left Barry's face. Adeline blinked, looking as if somebody had thrown a bucket of cold water on her.

Adeline clutched Barry's arm. "But he told you he couldn't make any more contributions this year. He lied to you, Barry!"

"Of course, he lied!" Barry snarled. "He orchestrated this whole thing just to make me look like a fool."

As Albert began to talk about having his own architects draw up plans for the Albert Butterfield Wing, a sarcastic laugh escaped Adeline. "A million dollars?" she whispered to her husband. "To make you look foolish? Don't be ridiculous. You can manage that all by yourself."

"What is that supposed to mean?"

"That little walk you took yesterday, down the hall to a certain person's room."

Barry went white. Then, suddenly, he seemed to remember Tess's presence and hissed, "Be quiet, Adeline! We'll talk about this later."

Chapter 12

"How could she do this to me?" wailed Hyacinthe Forrest as she made her way through the crush of customers who were crammed into the Queen Street Book Shop to join Tess at the front window.

"Still no sign of her," Tess murmured. Her gaze swept the people strolling down Queen Street. The block where the bookshop was located contained most of Victoria Springs's upscale shops and boutiques. Across the street was a store that carried designer-label dresses, a few of them one-of-a-kind and priced accordingly. South of that was a lace shop, a store with sparkling displays of fine china and glassware in its window and an antique store. Tess enjoyed browsing the Queen Street shops when she could find the time, but she rarely bought anything. Although she was already making a living with the bed and breakfast, she was putting aside any money she could save against the lean winter months when the tourist trade dropped off.

Beside Tess, Cinny twitched anxiously. "It's almost two-thirty," she said, as if Tess, too, hadn't been looking at her watch every three minutes. If one overlooked the flash of ire in Cinny's blue eyes, she looked like a sunny summer day in a pink-and-pale green cotton dress. She tucked a long strand of blond hair behind one ear and crossed her arms—to keep from wringing her hands, Tess supposed. Cinny, usually late for appointments herself, had little tolerance for people who kept *her* waiting. But in this case, Francine was keeping over a hundred people waiting.

"Could she have forgotten the signing?" Cinny whispered.

"I hardly think so. At breakfast this morning, she talked of little else. She was looking forward to it."

Cinny glanced unhappily over her shoulder. "I could strangle Francine. The customers are getting tired of waiting. They'll start to leave any minute and I'll be stuck with boxes of Francine's books."

Tess followed her gaze. Francine's former classmates waited in restless clusters around the shop. Ordinarily a cozy oasis of walnut paneling, floor-to-ceiling shelves of books and conveniently placed chairs and benches for customers who wanted to tarry for a bit, the bookshop seemed about to burst at the seams this afternoon.

Cinny's mother stood in one corner talking to Rachel Waller and Rachel's mother and sister. Until a few minutes ago, Tess had never met Rachel's family. Rachel stood out like a flawless diamond surrounded by cubic zirconias.

As Tess watched, Dahlia patted Coralee Leander's arm and excused herself to join another group of people.

"Aunt Dahlia's mingling," Tess said. "Maybe we should do the same."

"Wait a minute!" Cinny leaned closer to the window. "There she is. Oh, thank goodness!"

Tess saw Francine get out of her rented Ford at the end of the block and hurry toward the shop. Another car screeched around the corner on two wheels and weaved back and forth, barely missing several tail lights as the driver looked for a parking place. Tess recognized Rita De-'Lane at the wheel. Was it possible the woman was just learning to drive? She probably couldn't read a road map, either. No wonder it had taken so long for her to find Victoria Springs.

Finding no empty parking spaces on the block, Rita

squealed around the corner and out of sight. Just as Francine reached the bookshop, Rita appeared at the corner on foot and hurried after her.

Francine rushed into the shop. "I'm terribly sorry to be so late."

Cinny was so exasperated with the author by that time that she gave Francine a withering look, turned without a word, and headed for the cash register counter to join her clerk, Belva Hooker, who had spent the half hour they'd been waiting for Cinny gossiping and speculating with customers about Francine's new book. Clearly she was trying to find out if anybody knew more than she did about the subject matter. From what Tess had heard of the conversations, nobody did.

"We were beginning to worry about you, Francine," Tess said.

"I made the mistake of going back to Iris House after spending the morning writing at the library," Francine whispered. "I knew if I stayed at Iris House that woman would give me no peace. But when I got back to the house, she was waiting for me. She held me prisoner in my room, trying to make me say I wouldn't leave her agency."

"How did she hold you prisoner?" Tess asked doubtfully. Francine must outweigh Rita De'Lane by twenty or thirty pounds.

"She grabbed my car keys off the dresser and wouldn't give them back. But I showed her!" Tess imagined a scuffle over the keys, but now was not the time to ask more questions.

Francine faced the crowd and raised her voice. "Thank you all for coming, and for waiting. I apologize for being late, but I was unavoidably detained."

When Tess looked back toward the front of the shop, she saw Rita standing near the door. Rita had slipped into the shop quietly, not her usual manner of making an appearance. She was dressed in a white skirt so mini it could barely be seen below a red knit tunic with leather sandals and white-striped hose with sheer insets. On her painted and powdered face, Rita wore a look of steely-eyed determination.

Ye gods, Tess thought and vowed silently to keep Rita away from Francine during the signing.

Dahlia had already settled Francine at the Queen Anne desk, which held stacks of her books, and a line of autograph-seekers was forming. Rita moved to a wall of books and began scanning titles. She seemed content to keep her distance from Francine for now. Tess took a deep breath and moved through the crowd retrieving napkins and cups and carrying them to the workroom, which was at the back of the shop with a tiny rest room.

A few minutes later, Tess joined Dahlia at the refreshment table that they'd set up in an alcove where the children's books were shelved.

In her fifties, Dahlia, in a white, eyelet dress, was still a beauty. As usual, every frosted hair was in place. She looked as if she'd just stepped out of the beauty parlor, though Tess knew for a fact that she had her hair done on Fridays. Dahlia had once told Tess that the secret to keeping her hair perfectly coiffed was satin pillow cases.

"For a while there," Dahlia said, "I thought we had a disaster on our hands. I can't imagine anything ruder than being late for your own autograph party. Poor Cinny was on the verge of tears." The one sure way to get Dahlia's dander up was to hurt her only child. Dahlia and her lawyer husband, Maurice, had almost given up on having children when Cinny came along. Not surprisingly, they'd spoiled her.

As for Cinny being on the verge of tears, Tess thought her cousin had looked more like she wanted to attack Francine. "I think Francine was talking to her agent," Tess said.

Dahlia slid her dark eyes toward the bank of books where Rita still stood. "Is that the woman in that dreadful getup?"

Tess nodded. "Help me keep an eye on her, will you?

If she gets anywhere near Francine, she'll start a scene."

"Over my dead body," Dahlia murmured. Looking hard at Rita, she added, "Or somebody's."

Which, as it turned out, was an unfortunate thing to have said.

Tess spent the next hour chatting with customers and serving refreshments from the lace-covered table in the alcove.

The Wilhelms, she noticed, watched Albert Butterfield most of the time as one former classmate after another came up to exclaim over Albert's magnanimous contribution to their alma mater.

Once she heard Barry say to his wife, "If I get elected to the Senate, I'll find a way to make his life miserable. I swear I will!"

"*I hate the little S.O.B.!*" Adeline muttered in response.

Whatever Barry had told Adeline about his visit to Francine's room had evidently satisfied her. At least, she no longer seemed angry with him. The two were joined now in their mutual fury at Albert Butterfield.

Several times, Albert looked their way and smiled devilishly. *He might as well stick his tongue out at them*, Tess thought.

Ted, Rachel, and Rachel's mother and sister, Jane, were next in line to get their books signed.

Tess rejoined Dahlia at the refreshment table. "I think Francine could use a cup of punch," she said.

Adeline appeared in front of them. "Could ah have some punch for Albert Butterfield?"

Tess looked up in surprise. Adeline's mouth had a sulky set to it. Why did she want to take punch to Albert—a man she said she hated? Perhaps she hoped Albert would take it as a peace offering and reconsider funding Barry's campaign. Oh, well, hope springs eternal . . .

Dahlia poured punch into two cups and handed one to Adeline. As she put the second cup in Tess's hand, she said, "For Francine, and tell her to sign three books for me."

Adeline headed toward the spot where Albert had been standing and Tess made her way to the desk where Francine sat. She'd almost reached Francine when Adeline spoke at her elbow. "Have you seen Albert?"

"He was right over there a minute ago."

"He's not now," Adeline said. Suddenly she thrust her cup at Tess. "I've changed my mind, anyway. Would you dispose of this?"

"Sure." Tess took the cup.

"You looked thirsty," she said to Francine as she set a cup on the desk.

Francine was autographing a book for Jane Leander and barely looked up. "Oh—thank you, Tess," she said as she finished the inscription.

"Aunt Dahlia wants you to sign three books for her."

Francine made a quick note on the pad of paper beside her and looked up to smile at the next person in line.

"Anybody want more punch?" Tess asked, holding up the extra cup.

"I'll take it," said a man who was four or five people back in the autograph line.

Handing him the cup, Tess turned around and almost ran into Rita De'Lane. "Rita, please don't make a scene here," she pleaded.

"I wouldn't dream of it." Rita sniffed and brushed past Tess.

"I'll believe that when pigs fly," Tess muttered to herself. She watched as Rita reached the desk, skirted it, and took up a position behind Francine where she folded her arms and leaned back against a bookshelf. If Francine knew Rita was there, she gave no indication of it and, for the moment, Rita seemed only interested in standing and watching. Maybe she wanted to keep Francine in her sights so that she could latch on to her when the autographing was finished.

The door to the back room opened and Albert Butterfield came out. He must have been in the rest room when Adeline had been looking for him. Tess glanced once more at Rita, who hadn't moved. She decided it was safe to turn her back.

Now the Wilhelms had joined the autograph-seekers. Tess noticed that they carefully avoided Albert's gaze.

She made her way back to the alcove and the refreshment table, stopping once to talk to the owner of the antique store across the street, who'd slipped in to buy a book and leave it for Francine to autograph when she got to it. After a few minutes, Tess left the antique store owner to conduct her business and was immediately stopped again by a couple she'd met at the dinner-dance the previous evening. They wanted to talk about Albert Butterfield and the success he'd made of his life since leaving Victoria Springs.

Tess extricated herself from the gushing couple as soon as politeness allowed. She went to the cash register counter where Cinny was ringing up sales. Belva Hooker was taking more of Francine's books from below the counter and stacking them on top.

"Did you hear," Belva whispered to Tess, "that Albert Butterfield wouldn't make a contribution to the high school unless they agreed to name the new wing after him?"

Tess shook her head, though she wasn't surprised.

"Now, I'm not one to judge," Belva muttered, "but if you ask me that sounds more like pride than generosity."

"Hmmm," Tess murmured and turned away from the gossipy Belva. She saw Luke come into the shop. He smiled and waved, and she went to meet him. Later, she would estimate that about fifteen minutes had passed between the time she'd left the punch on the desk for Francine and the moment she reached Luke.

That was the moment when a woman screamed.

"Francine?" another woman's voice queried shrilly. "Francine!"

Luke craned to see over the heads of customers. "What's going on back there? Where's Francine?"

"At the desk—" As Tess uttered the words, a crack appeared in the crush of people and she could see the desk. Francine was no longer seated there.

"She just sort of slid out of the chair," said a woman.

"She fainted!" a man said.

A second commanding male voice ordered, "Stand back, everybody. Give her some air." It was the man who'd acted as emcee at last night's dinner-dance.

"Let me through," demanded Peaches Martin. Tess recognized the voice from last evening, though she couldn't see the short woman. Evidently Peaches was trying to help Francine. "I can't wake her up. Francine!"

"She's having a convulsion!"

"Is she epileptic?"

"I don't know."

"Somebody look in her purse. Maybe she has some pills."

Luke charged through the bookshop with Tess in his wake. Tess spotted Cinny at the cash register. She was standing on tiptoe, trying to see what was going on.

Clucking, Belva hurried over to join the crowd around Francine. Dahlia, who was standing beside Cinny, grabbed the telephone. "I'm calling 911," she said.

When Tess and Luke reached the desk, a woman was rummaging through Francine's handbag. "There's nothing here," she wailed. "Not even an aspirin tablet."

A circle had formed around Francine, who lay writhing on the floral carpet.

"Oh, my word. Did you ever—?" That was Belva's shocked voice.

Peaches and a man were trying to keep Francine from hitting herself with her flailing arms. Most of the others seemed stunned into paralysis. Rachel stood with her arm around her mother. She appeared to be trying to calm Coralee, who had turned ashen. Rachel's sister, Jane, on the other side of her mother, hugged herself and looked away from Francine. Rita De'Lane and Albert Butterfield stood side by side. Rita repeatedly drove agitated fingers through her close-cropped hair. Albert stood rigid and stone-faced. It was impossible to tell what he was feeling. Barry Wilhelm's arm was around his wife, who had turned her back on Francine and buried her face in her husband's shirt. Ted Ponte kept rubbing his eyes, as though to wipe away tears—or the sight of Francine's agony.

"Somebody hand me a pencil or pen," Luke said as he and Tess pushed through the circle and knelt on either side of Francine. A woman standing in the circle of spectators got a ballpoint pen from her purse and handed it to Luke, who pushed it between Francine's teeth to keep her from biting her tongue.

Peaches Martin and the man who'd been helping her hold Francine's arms moved back to let Tess and Luke take over.

"What is *wrong* with her?" Peaches wailed. "How could she get so sick so fast?" Francine's eyes were closed, but her eyelids trembled and her arms and legs jerked spasmodically.

Nobody attempted to answer Peaches's questions.

Tess caught one of Francine's flailing arms. With her other hand, she smoothed Francine's brow. She's sick enough to die, Tess thought. "An ambulance is on the way, Francine. Can you hear me?"

Suddenly, Francine's body arched—once, twice, three times until the spasms were coming so quickly her body was almost continuously in an arched-back position. Tess knew Francine had to be in terrible pain. She had never felt so sorry for anyone in her life.

Luke raised his head. "Everybody outside," he said quietly. Stunned faces stared back at him. "Out on the sidewalk. Now. Don't talk, and go as quietly as you can."

They left in a surprisingly orderly manner, considering the circumstances. Only Tess, Luke, Dahlia, Cinny, and Belva Hooker remained in the shop.

Cinny's eyes were red. "She was sick all along," she said unsteadily. "That's probably why she was late. And I was rude to her. I didn't even speak to her when she came in."

Belva looked down in horror at Francine. "I've never seen anything like that in my life. How long can she keep doing that?"

Tess shook her head and glanced at Luke. "What else can we do for her?"

"Nothing. Wait for the paramedics."

"I feel so helpless," Tess wailed. Francine's arms were now rigid at her sides. Luke rose to his feet. Tess continued to kneel beside Francine's convulsing body. The cup that had contained Francine's punch lay shattered on the floor beneath the desk. She must have knocked it off when she fell.

Luke touched her shoulder. "I hear the ambulance. The medics will know what to do." He took Tess's arm as she stood reluctantly. She stumbled against him and, for a moment, he wrapped his arms around her tightly.

The bookshop door burst open and two medics rushed in. "She's back here," Tess called.

As the medics reached Francine, she fell on her side, still in the arched-back position, and stopped moving. Her eyes were wide open now, frozen in an expression of fear, and her face was set in a ghastly, open-mouthed contortion.

"Oh, no!" Cinny gasped. "I think she stopped breathing." Dahlia patted Cinny's shoulder and murmured soothing words.

"Let's all move back so they can work," Luke suggested. They clustered at the cash register counter while the medics worked frantically over Francine's rigid body.

"She's not going to make it, is she?" Cinny asked, tears trickling down both cheeks.

A frown knitted Dahlia's brow. "If she has epilepsy, why didn't she have her pills with her?"

"Who said she has epilepsy?" Belva asked.

"I don't know—somebody," Dahlia said. "Convulsions can be caused by other things, of course. I just don't know . . ."

"I never heard of Francine having epilepsy," Belva said, "and I knew her when she was growing up."

"You know what it reminds me of?" Dahlia murmured.

"Francine?" Tess asked.

Dahlia nodded gravely. "Honey convulsed like that right before she died."

Honey, Dahlia's poodle, had died of poisoning two years previously when there had been several pet poisonings in Victoria Springs over a three-week period. Then the poisonings had stopped, but the poisoner was never caught.

Honey was short for Honeysuckle. Unlike Tess's father, Dahlia had followed the family tradition of naming female offspring, including pets, after flowers.

Dahlia's words had drawn everybody's eyes to her. "Who's Honey?" Belva asked.

"Mother's poodle," Cinny told her. "She was poisoned."

A few moments of glum silence followed this, then Luke asked, "How did Francine seem when she got here?"

"She was fine," Tess said.

Cinny was gazing reflectively at her mother. "How could Francine have been poisoned? She's been here for over an hour, and I don't think she's eaten anything since she got here."

"She had a cup of punch," Tess said. She glanced toward the medics just as one of them jumped up and ran back to the ambulance for a litter. The other medic adjusted the controls on a portable oxygen tank. An oxygen mask covered Francine's contorted face. She still wasn't moving.

The medics wore grim looks as they carried Francine out—it was obvious that they thought Francine's condition was critical. The ambulance sped away, siren wailing.

"Where's the cup she drank from?" Luke asked.

"Under the desk," Tess said. "It's broken. She must have knocked it off when she fell."

Luke frowned. "We shouldn't touch it, or anything else around the desk. The police will want to secure the scene."

The police. Oh, dear, that meant Desmond Butts.

At the very moment Tess's mind formed the thought, the bookshop door was flung open and Desmond Butts, Chief of the Victoria Springs Police Department, lumbered inside. "Don't anybody leave," he yelled over his shoulder. "I may want a statement from every last one of you. I'll tell you when you can go." Butts liked to establish who was boss the minute he arrived at a crime scene.

He stalked toward the cluster of people at the cash register counter. His square face was red, his nostrils flared. His eyes swept the faces turned apprehensively toward him and stopped on Dahlia. His nod was barely perceptible. "Miz Forrest." He moved on to Cinny and Tess. "Miss Forrest and Miss Darcy. Some of the same bunch who were involved in that murder last spring."

"We were not *involved*," Tess protested. Luke caught her eye and shook his head. Arguing with Desmond Butts was an exercise in futility. She knew that, but she couldn't help it. "Besides, this isn't murder. It can't be."

Butts held up both hands for silence. "I got the medics on the car phone on the way here. It looks like a poisoning to them. 'Course it's not officially a poisoning until the medical examiner says so. I'll know for sure tomorrow."

Tess glanced at Dahlia, who was intently studying her smooth, clasped hands.

"Now," Butts snarled, "will somebody tell me what in blue blazes happened this time?"

Chapter 13

Desmond Butts jerked a handkerchief from the hip pocket of his uniform and swiped his sweaty brow, then resettled his glasses on the broad bridge of his nose. After phoning the hospital and learning they had been unable to revive Francine, he'd begun to perspire profusely. Francine's body was being moved to the morgue.

Butts had spent half an hour questioning Tess, Luke, Cinny, Dahlia, and Belva. Who was close to Francine when she collapsed? Had she left the room at any time since her arrival? Had she said anything about feeling unwell? Had they seen anybody touch the cup she drank from while it was sitting on the desk?

Along with the others, Tess answered these questions in a few, carefully chosen words. She merely shook her head when Butts asked finally, in frustration, if anybody had seen or heard *anything* suspicious. Tess had seen and heard all kinds of suspicious—or, at least, puzzling—things since Sunday, and she and Dahlia had definitely touched the cup. But it was too complicated to go into at that moment. She would try to explain everything in due time.

Officer Andy Neill had arrived at the bookshop shortly after Butts, summoned by the chief as he was

118

en route. Neill, a shy, gangly young man with a sandy forelock that kept falling into his gray-green eyes and unfortunate jug ears, had bagged the broken punch cup and was now following the chief's terse instructions to sketch the scene.

Butts stuffed the handkerchief back in his pocket and grunted as his eyes skipped over the small group gathered inside the shop, including the ones he'd just called back in from the sidewalk. They were perspiring, too, having been kept standing in the hot sun for nearly an hour.

Butts cleared his throat and pinned Tess with his hazel eyes, small pebbles set in an expanse of ruddy flesh. If ever she had seen eyes that could accurately be described as "beady," they were Desmond Butts's.

"Miss Darcy, you seem to attract death like molasses draws ants." His voice boomed sonorously in the bookshop.

Tess felt herself bristling. Desmond Butts usually managed to put her on the defensive whenever their paths crossed. Luke said it was because she was a Darcy, and Butts, who'd grown up in abject poverty, resented those with more money or influence than he. Tess had pointed out that everything she had was in Iris House, but Luke said to Butts that looked like a lot. She made an effort to give Butts the benefit of his upbringing and did not comment on his accusatory remark. Instead, she crossed her arms and pressed her lips together to trap unwise words before they could be uttered.

Butts went on. "And from what you've said, you took more notice than anybody else of the people who were close to Francine Alexander when she collapsed. Why is that?" He managed to sound as if he thought she were hiding a bottle of poison on her person. "Were you expecting trouble?"

How could she explain that she'd had an uneasy sense of impending trouble ever since Sunday afternoon's tea in the library? Should she mention that Rita De'Lane had followed Francine to the bookshop after keeping her in her room until she was late to the autographing and that she, Tess, had been more watchful than the others because she feared Rita would create another scene, like the one last night at the high school? Or that Francine's old school chums had been worried about the book Francine was writing?

Tess opened her mouth, then had second thoughts. There would be time enough when and if evidence was found that a murder had been committed. Until she knew for sure, she would cling to the hope that Francine's death could be ascribed to a natural cause.

"No, I wasn't expecting trouble," Tess said. "I was looking for people who'd finished their refreshments so I could relieve them of their empty plates and cups."

Butts stared at her, as though he suspected every word she uttered was a lie. Tess stared back.

Butts's heavy face reddened, and he swept his arm toward the small assemblage of people. "Are you sure they're all here, the ones you say were close to Francine Alexander when she fell out of her chair? Look 'em over. See if you can think of anyone else."

Tess gazed thoughtfully at the people Butts had brought back in from the sidewalk. Albert Butterfield had huffily taken up a position a little apart from the others. He had removed his linen sport jacket and tossed it over a chair. His shirt was damp under the arms, and his hands were thrust into his trouser pockets, his light brows drawn together in a thoroughly disgruntled frown. Plainly he thought he was too important to be detained with a group of nobodies by the police.

Rita De'Lane perched on a chair near the cash register counter, her legs crossed, one sandaled foot jiggling agitatedly. She'd smeared her mascara, wiping her perspiring face with a paper napkin. Beneath the remaining paint and powder, her face was haggard, and Tess realized that Rita was older than she had guessed initially—in her late forties, probably. Perhaps feeling Tess's gaze, Rita looked up sharply, reminding Tess of a startled animal.

Rachel Waller huddled with her mother and sister on a bench that had been pushed back against a bank of books to make room for the Queen Anne desk. Her face was pale, whether from shock or something else, Tess couldn't tell. Coralee Leander appeared troubled as she repeatedly darted glances at Rachel. In contrast, Jane's plain face wore a completely bewildered look.

Ted Ponte, his expression grim, stood beside the bench near Rachel, one elbow propped on a bookshelf, giving Tess the impression that he wanted to be close enough to protect her should she need it.

The Wilhelms sat straight and close together on an ottoman which, like the bench, had been pushed out of the way against a wall of books. A blue vein pulsed in Barry's temple. Adeline made a face and pulled the front of her dress away from her damp skin with two fingers. When Tess's eye caught Adeline's, she looked away uneasily, which reminded Tess of something she'd momentarily forgotten. While she was still holding Francine's punch, Adeline had handed her another cup of punch meant for Albert. Which cup had Tess set on the desk for Francine?

That was something she would have to think about later.

Dahlia, Cinny and Belva were near the cash register. Dahlia was clearly worried. Belva's darting eyes were alert and curious. Cinny looked downright sick.

Tess swallowed. "When Francine became ill, Aunt Dahlia was in the alcove at the other end of the store, where the refreshment table is. Cinny and Belva were near the cash register, about where they are now. When I brought Francine the cup of punch—"

"Hold it right there," Butts interrupted sharply. "Where did you get the punch?"

"From the punch bowl on the refreshment table."

"You dipped it yourself?"

Tess glanced at Dahlia. "Well—"

"I dipped the punch and gave it to Tess, Chief," Dahlia

said firmly. "I've been serving punch all afternoon. Everybody here for the book-signing probably had some of that punch at one time or another."

Butts lifted a bushy eyebrow, which made him look as if a huge spider were crawling up his forehead. "Go on, Miss Darcy."

"As I was saying, Aunt Dahlia stayed in the alcove with the refreshments. When I brought the punch to Francine, I think Cinny and Belva were behind the counter." She looked at Cinny for confirmation, and Cinny nodded. "The others here, except for Luke, were gathered around the desk where Francine was autographing. I gave her the punch and went back toward the front of the shop, stopping to talk to a few people on the way."

If necessary, she would tell him later about the second cup of punch, the one Adeline had handed to her—after she'd had time to sort it out for herself. "Then I saw Luke at the door and went to meet him. He arrived just before Francine collapsed." She wanted to be absolutely sure Butts understood that Luke was out of it.

Butts's beefy face scrunched together in thought. "How much time passed after you gave Francine Alexander the punch before she collapsed?"

Tess thought about it. "Fifteen minutes, I guess. Twenty minutes at the outside."

"And you're sure she didn't eat or drink anything except that punch you gave her?"

"I didn't see her eat anything else while she was in the bookshop," Tess said. "Did anybody?"

As heads moved in denial, Butts growled, "Please, Miss Darcy. I'll ask the questions here."

"Sorry," Tess said curtly.

"Hmmm," Butts pondered. "Is there anything else you want to tell me, Miss Darcy?"

Tess shook her head.

He swept a melancholy gaze over the others. "Anybody else?"

Nobody responded.

"Might as well be a bunch of deaf mutes," Butts barked. "All right. Depending on what the medical examiner finds on autopsy, I may need a statement from every one of you. Right now, I just want to know where I can find you tomorrow if I need to. I hope no one is planning to leave town before then." He watched them like a cat ready to land with all four feet, claws unsheathed, on the hapless individual who admitted to such a plan.

Again, no one spoke.

"Good." He took out a small spiral notebook and pen. As one after another said they were staying at Iris House, Butts shot Tess several narrow-eyed glances as if an opinion had been confirmed, that nefarious goings-on were the norm at the bed and breakfast.

When he'd finished writing, he slapped the cover closed on the notebook and returned it to his shirt pocket. "You can go now. If anybody tries to leave town, he'll be detained as a material witness. Miss Forrest, I'm afraid you'll have to close your shop until we know whether or not it's the scene of a crime."

"For how long?" Cinny asked, alarmed.

"I'll let you know as soon as I hear from the M.E. And leave everything just the way it is until I get back to you."

"But the dirty dishes—" Cinny began in protest.

"Leave 'em," Butts ordered and stomped out, followed by his young deputy.

The silence the officers left behind was ominous. It was Barry Wilhelm who finally broke it. "Can he really detain us if we try to leave town?"

"I wouldn't want to put him to the test," Luke said.

"Why?" Tess asked Barry. "Weren't you planning to stay until the reunion activities are over?"

He turned to Tess. Instead of answering her question, he said querulously, "I don't even know why Adeline and I were called back in here by the police. I suppose you included us in your list of suspects, Tess."

Albert expelled a long-suffering breath, and Barry shot him a look that would have melted a more timid man.

"I saw you come up to the desk when I gave Francine the punch," Tess explained. "And that's what I told Butts. Nobody said anything about suspects. For all we know, Francine died of a heart attack."

"None of us believes that," muttered Albert. The somber words hung in the air, and nobody contradicted them.

"Well, I for one wanted her alive," Rita De'Lane said shrilly, her darting look challenging the others to disagree with her.

"Ah can tell you're overcome by grief," sneered Adeline.

Rita whirled on her. "Damn straight. She isn't worth anything to the agency dead."

"I understood she was leaving your agency," Ted Ponte put in.

Rita reddened. "That was just talk. Francine was with us from the beginning of her career. Underneath it all, she was loyal to us. She would never have left."

Rachel laughed raggedly. "Francine loyal?"

Her mother said sharply, "Rachel!"

Rachel covered her face with trembling hands.

Belva Hooker came around the cash register counter to pat Rachel's shoulder and lean toward her solicitously. "You poor little thing. What did you mean by that remark, Rachel? What did Francine do to you? Far be it from me to be nosy, but it always helps to talk, you know."

Rachel merely shook her head miserably back and forth.

Ted Ponte stepped up, lifted Belva's hand from Rachel's shoulder and moved between the two women. "Get away from her. Leave her alone."

"Well! I was only trying to help," Belva retorted haughtily as she backed away.

"Can't you see she doesn't want your help?" Ted said.

Belva stormed back to the counter. "I will not stay here and be insulted, Cinny."

Cinny shrugged. "You might as well go home. We'll have to leave this mess until the chief says we can clean it up."

Muttering to herself, Belva got her purse and left the shop. But Tess was sure she wouldn't go home until she'd made the rounds of the business district, describing in gory detail what had happened in the bookshop. The others exchanged uncertain looks, as if nobody wanted to be the first to follow Belva. Finally, Rita De'Lane stood, smoothed her tunic, tugged on the hem of her miniskirt, and walked out. The others followed quickly.

Rita backed the rental car into the street. A pickup approaching from the south barely avoided slamming into her. The outraged driver rolled down his window and shook his fist.

"Redneck," she fumed and gave him the finger as she screeched around a corner. She hadn't driven for years before she picked up the rental car at the Springfield airport. Even if she could afford a car, she couldn't afford to pay New York City parking fees. She hadn't been a good driver, even before she moved to Manhattan. She was always in too big of a hurry to get where she was going, and her mind was invariably on other things.

The narrow, crowded streets of Victoria Springs's business district made her as nervous as a long-tailed cat in a room full of rocking chairs.

Victoria Springs, Missouri, was like a foreign country to Rita. Ever since she arrived, she'd been tense enough to jump out of her skin. Her mind kept yelling at her, *Get me out of here*!

Calm down, Rita, she told herself. *Calm, calm.*

If she could get the damned car back to Iris House without doing major damage to it, she would park it and leave it there until she was allowed to depart this sorry excuse for a town. If she had to stay much longer, she would go stark, staring mad.

She cursed and jerked the steering wheel sharply to the right to avoid an oncoming Buick. The driver's eyes showed an incredible amount of white all around; she must have thrown the woman driver into shock. Well, it wasn't

entirely Rita's fault. These streets were barely wide enough
for two cars to pass. Of course, her depth perception did
leave something to be desired. She was never sure she
hadn't let a wheel wander over the center line.

She vowed fervently never to drive a car again. Taxis
were invented for people like Rita. Unfortunately, they
didn't have taxis in Victoria Springs, Missouri.

Finally, she felt taut neck muscles relax a little as she
left the business district behind and entered a residential
area on a street that would eventually climb the hill to the
neighborhood of old Victorian houses where Iris House was
located.

Almost there, Rita. Stay calm.

Maybe she would be able to sleep tonight for a change.

Francine was dead. She savored the words in her mind
as a small smile curved her painted mouth. No more arguing and cajoling and threatening to sue Francine for
breach of contract to keep her from leaving the agency. No
more pampering and urging and lying to keep Francine at
her computer.

Best of all, her boss didn't know what had passed between her and Francine in Victoria Springs. She'd tell him
that Francine had apologized for interviewing other agents
on the sly and promised to keep the terms of her contract
before her sudden, unexpected death.

She might even be able to work up a credible display of
grief over Francine's unfortunate demise.

"Let's go up to Francine's room," Tess said, grabbing
Luke's hand. They had just arrived at Iris House from the
bookshop, and Tess had picked up the master key she kept
in her apartment. "I need your computer expertise." Luke
kept all his business records on computer. He was always
telling Tess that she had to join the computer age, book-
keeping was so much faster on computer. Tess knew he
was right, but she hadn't had time to do anything about it
yet. Maybe when she finished the quilting class, she'd en-
roll in a computer course.

Luke arched a blond brow, but followed her up the stairs. No one was in the hallway when Tess quietly unlocked the door of the Cliffs of Dover Room and they stepped inside.

Francine's laptop computer sat open on the small table beneath the window. Several pens and loose pieces of paper containing scribbled notes were scattered around it. Stacked on a corner of the table were a dictionary, thesaurus, and Bartlett's *Familiar Quotations*.

Tess gestured toward the chair that was pulled up to the table. "I want to know what's in that book she was writing," she explained. "Can you bring it up on the screen?"

Luke cocked his head. "I can, but should I?"

"Why not?"

"It could be tampering with evidence, Tess."

"How can it be tampering with evidence," Tess asked innocently, "when we don't even know that a crime has been committed?"

"A mere technicality, my dear," Luke said gravely. "Albert Butterfield was right, you know. You saw what happened. Francine's was no natural death."

"I'm not willing to accept that—yet. Meanwhile, I'm curious about the book that had everybody so uptight. Aren't you?"

Luke's eyes sparkled in spite of an obvious effort to remain sober. "Yes," he admitted.

"Well?"

He hesitated another moment, then chuckled. "Ok, you win, Tess." He sat down before the computer and turned it on. With Tess looking over his shoulder, his fingers flew across the keyboard.

"Hmmm," he murmured. "Not there. Let's try this . . . Nothing there, either. Hmmm."

Tess laid a hand on his shoulder and tapped her fingers impatiently. Luke typed, mumbled, and typed some more.

Finally, he dropped his hands from the keyboard. "That's it. Nothing."

"That's impossible. How can there be nothing?"

"The hard disk has been wiped clean."

"What! Are you sure?"

"Absolutely. Even the word-processing program is gone. Whoever did it took out everything."

"So," Tess pondered. "He wanted to make sure every bit of incriminating evidence was gone."

Luke nodded. "He or she. You're assuming this is connected to Francine's death?"

"It's possible," Tess said. "No, it's probable."

He stood and shuffled through the papers on the table. "There doesn't seem to be a hard copy of the manuscript, either. She should have made backups, though. Anybody who knows anything about computers copies up their documents on floppy disks."

"Those things I've seen in your office in the paper envelopes?"

"Right. Or she might have used the smaller disks. They ought to be in a square, plastic container. Her computer has drives for both sizes." He moved to the dresser and began going through drawers. "Check the closet, Tess. Maybe she kept them in there."

They went through everything in the room and the closet, but found no computer disks.

"It's possible she hadn't taken the time to do backups," Luke suggested finally. "A risky practice, that."

"She would never have chanced losing the book she kept saying would put her back on the best-seller lists." Tess shook her head. "No, whoever wiped the hard disk clean took the backups, too." She opened the door and examined its edge. "There are only two master keys," she said. "I have one and Nedra has the other. Whoever blanked out the computer disk had to break in." She ran her finger along the edge of the door. "There are no marks here, though."

Luke examined the locks. "When Francine wasn't in the room, neither the dead bolt nor the safety chain was engaged. The only lock in place was the one in the doorknob. A credit card would open that."

Tess promised herself to have better locks installed as

soon as possible. *A bit like buying a smoke alarm after the house has burned down*, she thought unhappily. "It could have happened any time this morning. Francine wasn't here."

She went back to the table where the computer sat. A torn piece of paper, used as a place marker, stuck out of *Bartlett's Familiar Quotations*. Tess opened the book to the place marked. Written on the piece of paper were enigmatic phrases:

Umpire of Men's Miseries
New-Risen From a Dream
Empty Tigers
Call Back Yesterday
Little Wrongs

"Looks like she was still searching for a title," Tess murmured. She closed the book and glanced through the other scribbled notes Francine had left. One was a list of names: *Tim, Ben, Regina, Fanny*. She handed it to Luke. "Do you know who these people are?"

Luke studied the note, shook his head, and handed it back to her. "Maybe they're characters in her novel."

Tess drew a quick breath. "Look. All the names start with the same letters as the names of Francine and her closest high school friends—the Four Musketeers they were called. Ted and Tim, Ben and Barry, Regina and Rachel, Fanny and Francine. That can't be coincidence."

Hurriedly, she scanned the other notes. *Expand character descriptions, Chap. 2. Change Regina's hair to black*, one said. Rachel's hair was blond. Maybe Francine had changed all her characters' physical descriptions to better disguise the real people on whom they were based.

Another note said, *Rework scene p. 92 to plant hint of R's problem in conversation with F.* Tess reread the words, wishing that Francine had made more explicit notes. If *R* stood for Regina, and if Regina was, in fact, Rachel, this indication of a problem was intriguing. But what problem?

It could have been something as trivial as an argument with her boyfriend.

A third scrap of paper contained several dates in the spring of 1975. Tess picked up a blank piece of paper and, using one of Francine's pens, jotted down the dates. She tucked the paper in the pocket of her white shirt, ignoring Luke's disapproving look. Francine had spent the past couple of days at the library, reading old newspapers. The dates might refer to issues containing pertinent information that Francine had intended to go back to later.

"Ted Ponte had dinner with Francine Sunday evening," Tess mused. "Maybe she told him what the book was about." She would ask Ted at the first opportunity.

"Let's get out of here," Luke said. "Looking through Francine's things makes me feel like a voyeur."

"All right," Tess agreed. There was nowhere left to look, anyway, and she didn't want one of the guests to see them in Francine's room. She wouldn't like to try to explain to Butts why they were going through Francine's notes.

In the Carnaby Room, Albert Butterfield shot the bolt and engaged the safety chain before he shrugged out of his jacket and pulled two floppy computer disks from his pocket. Clutching the disks close to his chest, he crossed to a window to gaze at a moist bed of yellow petunias in an expanse of lush, manicured green lawn. Cooled by the rented Lincoln's air-conditioning, he savored the warmth of the sunlight that streamed in a golden path through the glass pane and congratulated himself on his ingenuity.

Damn, he was good.

When Albert Butterfield set his mind to something, nothing short of a global disaster could stand in the way of his accomplishing it. No wonder he was such a whiz at making money.

Now he had Francine's book and, as soon as he could get to a computer, he'd find out how she'd depicted him. He hoped the fortuitous event of her death before she'd finished her magnum opus would put an end to any publication plans. But he hadn't gotten rich by hoping for the best. For all he knew, she'd completed a first draft before she died and had mailed it to herself in New York. An editor could clean it up and have it on the stands in weeks. The ghoulish American public being what it was—and the shameless publishing industry being what *it* was—the author's untimely death might even be turned into a publicity gimmick to boost sales. It wouldn't be the first time a piece of trash had been hyped to runaway best-sellerdom.

But if, as he suspected, he'd been portrayed in an unfavorable light, he'd stop publication cold with lawsuits. He'd charge libel and invasion of privacy and whatever else he and a clever lawyer could come up with. He could keep it in the courts for years, if necessary. But it wouldn't be. They'd crumble as soon as the papers were served. Publishers feared lawsuits more than a bad *New York Times* review.

He looked around for a hiding place secure enough to escape the notice of Butts and his bumbling Keystone Cops if they decided to search the house. With such superior brainpower on his side, it shouldn't be difficult. He considered and rejected several possibilities before he went to a corner of the room and worked his fingers down between the rose carpet and the wall. With one sharp tug, he loosened the corner of the carpet just enough to slip the computer disks underneath it. Then he tucked the loose section of carpet back into place.

Standing, he surveyed his handiwork. There was no visible bump. You couldn't tell the carpet in that corner had ever been tampered with. Those dim idiots would never think of looking there.

He flopped down on the bed. As soon as he got back to his Chicago office . . .

Then he remembered. *Oh, hell.* Butts the butt had told them not to leave town. For the time being, he was stuck in this tacky burg.

Well, at least there was Thursday's paper to look forward

to. Surely by the weekend they'd be allowed to leave. He'd never return, except perhaps for a single day, for the dedication of the Albert Butterfield Wing at the high school.

God, he'd be glad to see the last of this place.

Chapter 14

"Strychnine, Miss Darcy," bellowed Butts the next afternoon in the guest parlor of Iris House.

Shades of Agatha Christie, Tess thought. She wasn't exactly shocked that the medical examiner had found poison but, in spite of the discovery that Francine's book was no longer in her computer, Tess had hoped against hope that the autopsy would reveal some noncriminal explanation for Francine's sudden death.

"An ugly way to go." Butts's fleshy lips turned down in consternation. "Very ugly."

His words brought to Tess's mind the horrible memory of Francine's death throes. But his next words jerked her rudely back to the present.

"Do you have any strychnine on the premises?"

"No!"

Butts pushed up his glasses and pinched the bridge of his nose as if he had a headache. He resettled the glasses. "Then you'll have no objection to my men searching the place?"

"Of course not."

"I'll get a couple of officers on it."

"I suppose you want to take statements from my guests now."

"Don't rush me," Butts responded. "I'll take yours first along with your fingerprints. There were traces of strychnine on that broken cup and some good, clear prints, too.''

"You *should* find my prints on the cup,'' Tess said. "I've already told you I took the punch to Francine. You'll probably find Aunt Dahlia's there, too.''

"We'll see,'' he said noncommitally and added, "I don't want anybody in the room where Francine Alexander was staying until we have a chance to go over it.''

"All right,'' Tess agreed with utter innocence.

After he'd taken her prints, she answered his questions as truthfully as she could. She held almost nothing back, including the fact that Francine's former classmates staying in Iris House had seemed excessively concerned about the book Francine was writing. The one fact she kept to herself was that she and Luke had searched the Cliffs of Dover Room. Butts would discover soon enough that the hard disk in Francine's computer had been erased and there were no backup disks in the room.

When he'd finished with her, he said curtly, "Get Adeline Wilhelm down here.'' Butts's irritating way of ordering people around nettled, but Tess knew it would do no good to complain.

She fetched Adeline. Barry came, too. To lend Adeline moral support, Tess supposed, but Butts banished Barry from the parlor without discussion. When Tess started to follow Barry out, Butts barked, "You stay for a few minutes, Miss Darcy.''

It soon became clear why he wanted her there. Butts would see it as a case of the accuser facing the accused.

Adeline sat alertly on the edge of a chair and watched Butts warily.

Butts pulled over another chair and sat down facing Adeline. "Now, Miz Wilhelm,'' said Butts in a soft, nonthreatening tone that immediately put Tess on guard. "Why don't you tell me about that cup of punch you gave Miss Darcy in the bookshop.''

Adeline placed both hands over her mouth and blinked to keep back tears. "I want my husband here with me.''

"Can't you speak for yourself?" Butts inquired in a tone that indicated she was some kind of bimbo if she said no.

"Of course . . . only, I—I don't know what you're talking about."

Butts pointed a blunt finger at Tess. "Tell her what you told me."

"Adeline," Tess said, "when I was getting Francine's punch, you asked Aunt Dahlia to pour another cup. You said it was for Albert Butterfield, but a few minutes later, you said you'd changed your mind and handed it to me. I was standing near the autographing desk at the time. Surely you remember that."

Adeline's only response was a quick back-and-forth shake of her head.

Butts leaned forward so that his face was virtually nose-to-nose with Adeline's. "We can always continue this at the station, Miz Wilhelm. Maybe you'd like to call your lawyer."

"Lawyer?" She leaned back, putting distance between herself and Butts. "Ah don't need a lawyer."

Butts erupted from his chair. "Then maybe you need a hypnotist," he growled, "to help you remember what happened this afternoon."

"No." Adeline said in a small voice. "It's beginning to come back to me now. Ah guess it happened about like Tess says it did." She slid a frightened glance in the chief's direction. "It was so unimportant, you see, that ah couldn't remember at first."

Butts scratched his chin. "Yeah, right."

"You can't think—ah mean, that's not the cup Francine drank from . . ." She looked pleadingly at Tess.

"It seems," Butts muttered, "that Miss Darcy has forgotten which cup she gave to Francine Alexander. Like you forgot you'd given her that cup of punch. Sure seems like there's a lot of forgetfulness going around."

"I'm sorry, Adeline," Tess said. "I really am not sure which cup I handed to Francine."

"Ah don't see what difference it makes," Adeline said

to the chief. "You aren't even sure she was—was murdered, are you?"

"I am now. Somebody slipped strychnine in her punch," Butts said sternly. "This is a murder investigation, Miz Wilhelm."

"But it has nothing to do with me," Adeline insisted. "The cup I gave Tess contained punch, nothing else."

"And you were going to give it to Butterfield?" Butts inquired in a disbelieving tone. "Miss Darcy overheard you saying you hated the man. Are you sure you want to stick to that story?"

Adeline gave Tess an offended look, and Tess shrugged helplessly.

"You still say you were taking that punch to Butterfield?" Butts pressed.

Adeline drew in a deep breath. "Yes, I was. I—I was so mad at him for the way he treated Barry that I was going to throw the punch on his expensive linen jacket—and pretend it was an accident." She looked down. "I know it sounds childish, and it was. Fortunately, I couldn't find him right away."

"He must have been in the rest room at the back of the shop," Tess inserted. "I saw him come out of the back room after I took the punch from Adeline."

"Anyway," Adeline went on, "it gave me time to realize how petty ah was being. Ah was lowering myself to his level. So ah gave the punch to Tess."

"Dispose of it, I believe you told her," Butts put in.

"Ah can't remember exactly what ah said, but something like that."

"Interesting choice of words," Butts snorted.

"Ah only meant she should take the cup back to the refreshment table," Adeline insisted.

"Miz Wilhelm, do you really expect me to believe you, a sophisticated woman, got that punch to throw it on Albert Butterfield? Tell the truth, ma'am. Didn't you mean that cup for Francine Alexander all along? And didn't you doctor it up before—"

"No!" For the first time, Adeline seemed to realize how it could easily look that way. "Why would I want to poison Francine?"

"Maybe because she and your husband were getting a little too chummy. Didn't he visit her in her room alone Sunday night?"

"How did you—" She looked at Tess and evidently realized from Tess's expression that Tess knew of Barry's clandestine visit to Francine and had told Butts. "Oh, Lord." Adeline's hands fluttered in her lap and a nervous giggle escaped her. "Ah wasn't jealous of that fat slob! Oh, ah'm sorry. Ah didn't mean—What ah meant to say was you'll have to ask Barry what he was doing in Francine's room."

"Don't worry. I intend to," Butts snapped. Tess had repeated what she had heard of the conversation to Butts. It would be interesting to know if Barry's version of it jibed with hers.

"All ah know is ah didn't put any poison in the punch ah handed to Tess!" Adeline looked at Butts and blinked her big blue eyes. "You have to believe me!"

"Maybe I'll believe you when you tell me the truth, Miz Wilhelm. That story about taking the punch to Albert Butterfield and then changing your mind doesn't hold water."

"But that's what happened! Ah was very angry with Albert. Ah still am. He said he couldn't contribute to Barry's campaign because he'd already given his limit in charitable contributions this year . . . for tax purposes, I guess he meant. Anyway, it was a lie because he turned right around and gave a million dollars to build a wing on the high school."

"You're just digging a deeper hole for yourself," Butts told her. "After all that, you wouldn't have wanted to carry punch to Albert Butterfield—and don't give me that story about throwing it on his jacket. You wouldn't want to give Butterfield anything—not unless you knew the punch was poisoned."

"No, no, no!" Adeline shook her head back and forth. "Albert kept looking at Barry and me and sneering, and ah got so mad, ah just—well, ah already told you what I meant to do, and it's no story. It's the truth, ah swear! Ah changed my mind, that's all."

Butts paced across the parlor glowering. Turning back, he frowned at Tess. "You can leave now, Miss Darcy. If you should happen to recover your memory about which cup you gave Francine Alexander—"

"Naturally, I'll tell you right away," Tess said.

As she closed the parlor door, Butts said, "Now, Miz Wilhelm, let's start from the beginning." Tess's sympathy was with Adeline.

Tess went to her apartment and phoned Nedra, who'd gone home for the day. She gave her the news that Francine had died of strychnine poisoning.

"Lord have mercy," Nedra muttered.

"Nedra, I wouldn't even know where to get strychnine, would you?" Tess asked.

"Comes from a tree, I think," Nedra said, "grows in South America or India—somewhere foreign like that. Not here."

Nedra must have picked up that information from a book. She had recently become a fan of mystery novels.

"Used to put it in rat poison," Nedra was saying. "Don't think they do that any more. Oh—" She halted and Tess heard her sharp intake of breath.

"What's wrong?"

"Just wondering if Miss Iris left any old rat poison around."

Not in the house, Tess thought. She'd cleaned every nook and cranny when the house was being renovated. "I'd have found it by now," she said. "I wanted to ask you, though, if you saw anyone near Francine's room while you were cleaning upstairs today."

"Everybody."

"You saw several people in Francine's room?"

"Didn't say that. I saw everybody who's staying there *near* Francine's room. That's what you asked, isn't it?"

"Yes," Tess sighed, wishing Nedra wouldn't be quite so literal. "What do you mean? You saw them going in, coming out, what?"

"No, just near, like I said. You walk down the upstairs hall, you're near that room. That's all I meant."

"So you saw them all in the hall at one time or another today?"

"Yep. Saw that New York woman more'n once, slinking around. Rigged out like it was Halloween. All the other guests went by once or twice, too. Few other people besides. Woman from the paper looking for Barry Wilhelm. He and the Missus was out. Mrs. Leander and Jane came to get Rachel for the book party—"

This was an unusually long speech for Nedra. She stopped abrupty as though she'd run out of breath.

"What did the woman from the paper want?" Tess asked.

"Doing an article," Nedra said. "Said she wanted a coat—or something like that. Didn't make much sense."

"A quote?"

"Yeah, that coulda been it."

"Did you leave the door to Francine's room open for any length of time while you were somewhere else?"

"Yep. Had to go downstairs for more linen, didn't I? Left my cart in the door, though."

Which wouldn't have prevented anyone's going into the room, Tess mused.

"Didn't you say Francine was poisoned at the bookshop?" Nedra asked.

"Yes."

"Then why are you so all-fired interested in who was near her room?"

"I can't explain now," Tess said. "Thanks for your help, Nedra."

After hanging up the phone, Tess stretched out on the

couch in the sitting room and closed her eyes. The events of the day had worn her out. She was getting drowsy when she was attacked by fifteen pounds of feline.

"Oafff," she grunted, startled wide-eyed as Primrose jumped on her stomach and settled down for a snooze. Tess chuckled and stroked Primrose's soft fur. Primrose purred loudly.

"You were less trouble when you ignored me," Tess told her. Upon her Aunt Iris's death a year ago, she had inherited the cat along with the house. For weeks, Primrose's attitude toward the interloper had been haughty disdain when she wanted to be fed and obliviousness the rest of the time. With patience on Tess's part, Primrose had finally come around to accepting that Tess was there to stay.

Closing her eyes again, Tess thought back to the moment that afternoon in the bookshop when Adeline had handed her the cup of punch. She'd still had the other cup in her right hand and had taken Adeline's cup with her left. She had been standing by the desk with her right side toward it, and she had leaned over and set one cup on the desk for Francine. It would have been awkward, in the crush of people, to reach across the desk with her left hand. Which meant she must have given Francine the cup in her right hand, the one originally intended for Francine. She gave the other cup to a man who was standing in the autograph line.

She went through it again in her mind. She was almost certain now that she had not given Francine the cup that Adeline handed her. Since the poison had not been in the punch bowl—a hundred people had drunk from it—it had been added to Francine's cup while it sat on the desk. That's the only way it could have happened.

First, the killer had gotten rid of Francine's tell-all book by erasing it from the computer and taking the backup disks. But to be sure the story would never be told, he had to get rid of Francine. So he'd come to the bookshop with the poison in a vial or a small envelope—something that could have been secreted in his closed hand. Perhaps he'd leaned over the desk to say something to Francine, shielding the cup from view with his body while he poured the poison into the cup.

A well thought-out and executed plan. Premeditated murder.

Except for Coralee and Jane Leander, neither of whom would seem to have a motive for murder, the people who had been close enough to Francine to add the poison to her punch were in Iris House at this very moment. *Which* of Iris House's beautiful rooms harbored a killer?

The answer may have been in Francine's missing book. What on earth had she been about to reveal?

In her wandering around town the last few days, "soaking up atmosphere," talking to people, had Francine let some vital piece of information slip out? Where had she gone and to whom had she talked? From what Francine had said, she'd spent a good deal of that time at the library.

Tess sat up abruptly, dislodging Primrose from her comfortable perch. The cat shook herself, leaped gracefully into her favorite chair, curled up, and was immediately asleep again.

Tess grabbed her purse and left her apartment by way of the side door. She was going to read the local newspapers of twenty years ago, beginning with the dates she'd copied from the note in Francine's room.

It was, at least, a starting place.

Her thoughts gave her brief pause. She was doing it again, she realized—undertaking her own investigation of a murder. Luke would say she should tell the police and let them look through the old newspapers.

But would they have the time for a lengthy look at the library's microfilm files? Except for about three months in the dead of winter, the tourist traffic in Victoria Springs strained the local officers' on-duty time to its limits. A murder investigation might take top priority, but there were only so many officers and so many hours in the day.

Besides Butts sometimes treated her like a half-wit. Tess wasn't at all sure that he would consider her hunches important enough to pursue.

Chapter 15

Jane Leander was at the checkout desk when Tess entered the library. "Hello, Tess," she said solemnly, gesturing Tess over to her. "How are you holding up?"

"All right," Tess said, "in spite of the fact that I was just grilled and fingerprinted by Chief Butts. At the moment, he's doing the same to my guests."

"I imagined he'd do that today. Butts called the apartment this morning and told Mother the medical examiner had found poison. He's coming to the apartment to talk to us this evening." She looked glum. "I almost didn't go to the book signing. The head librarian didn't like the idea of my being off all afternoon, but it turned out we weren't busy, so she finally told me to go ahead. I wish now that she hadn't." Her bland composure cracked a little. "I'll never forget seeing Francine like that."

"None of us will."

"My mother has always been so strong, but she's not handling Francine's death at all well. She hardly slept last night and when she did she had nightmares. She said she kept seeing Francine die over and over."

"It's bound to be harder on the people who knew Francine all her life."

Jane nodded. "When Rachel was in high school, Francine was at our house half the time. I was still

143

in elementary school and Rachel and Francine seemed so grown-up to me. I tried to tag along wherever they went. Made a real pest of myself, but Francine was always nice to me. She'd fix my hair and show me how to put on makeup. I don't remember all of it myself. My mother has told me about it.'' Her voice wavered and she looked down. With ringless, short-nailed fingers, she squared up a stack of memo pads and arranged the ballpoint pens next to the pads in a neat row.

Tess could hardly imagine retiring Jane Leander making a pest of herself; perhaps she'd been more outgoing as a child. But whatever hair and makeup hints Francine had given her had been wasted. Jane's hair was cropped short and held away from her face by a barrette on one side, and she used very little makeup.

"Jane," Tess said, "I understand Francine was here the last few days doing research. Do you know what she was researching?"

Jane knitted her brow. "She spent several hours reading old issues of the *Victoria Springs Gazette*. From the 1970s because the book she was writing took place then."

"Did she say what exactly she was looking for?"

Jane shook her head. "All she ever said was that she was refreshing her memory. You know she was using Victoria Springs as the model for the town in her book?" Tess nodded. "She read the *New York Times*, too, and took a lot of notes. She said she was getting a list of important national and world events to use as background material."

Tess did not remember seeing such a list among the notes in Francine's room. Maybe she'd put them on the computer and then threw away the handwritten notes she'd made at the library.

A distracted-looking woman, two toddlers in tow, came up to the desk with an armful of children's books. Tess said good-bye to Jane and took the stairs to the second floor where the newspaper files were kept. The reference librarian was busy, but Tess managed to find the microfilm cartridges containing the back issues of the local newspaper without any help.

She carried the two rolls that included the dates she'd copied from Francine's notes to a viewer, then threaded the one marked with the earlier dates on the film spool.

She quickly found the issue for March 25, 1975, the first date on the list Francine had made. The front page carried an article on a local woman who'd been named to a state education committee by the governor and another on a fifth-grader who was going to represent the local elementary school in the state spelling bee. A name in the short article at the bottom of the front page caught Tess's eye.

LOCAL MAN REPORTED MISSING, the headline read. Tess scanned the two paragraphs that followed.

> Ralph Leander, a resident of Victoria Springs for the past 23 years, was reported missing Monday by his wife, Coralee, according to police records. Contacted at home, Mrs. Leander said that her husband drove away from the house Sunday night and she hadn't heard from him since.
>
> "We don't start a search for a missing adult until they've been missing for at least 48 hours," said Officer Vince O'Hara of the Victoria Springs Police. "Usually they come back on their own by then." Wednesday the police launched a statewide search for Leander. As of press time, police had no leads, according to O'Hara.

Tess fed the machine a quarter and made a copy of the article. She went through the rest of the March 25 issue but found nothing else that she could connect to Francine, her friends, or the book she had been writing.

The second date on Francine's list was April 5, 1975. That issue of the local newspaper, on the same spool, carried a follow-up story on Ralph Leander's disappearance on the front page. According to the article, the search for Leander had been broadened to cover the nation, but the Victoria Springs chief of police was quoted as saying the few leads they'd received had led nowhere.

Neighbors of the Leanders, Olivia and Robert Perkins, had told the police they saw Leander drive away in his car Sunday evening and that the car "wandered all over the street," as though the driver were intoxicated. Reports of sightings of a gray Ford answering the description of Leander's Sunday night in a town forty miles to the west of Victoria Springs and another in the next county, almost 200 miles away, had led nowhere. There being no evidence of foul play, the police chief speculated that Leander had "deserted his family" and didn't want to be found. According to the article, Coralee Leander refused to comment on the speculation.

Tess made a copy of the article and quickly went through the remainder of the April 5 issue as well as the issues for the rest of April. Again, there was no mention of Francine or her high school classmates.

Tess rewound the spool, took it off the machine and threaded on the second roll of microfilm. The entire front page of the May 23 issue of the *Gazette*, the last date on Francine's list, covered the graduation ceremony at the local high school. The full text of valedictorian Albert Butterfield's speech took up the bottom half of the page. It contained the usual onward and upward sentiments of most such speeches. A reporter had interviewed several graduating seniors and their comments were included in the article at the top of the page.

Barry Wilhelm and Ted Ponte reported that they were already enrolled at the University of Missouri, Ponte on an athletic scholarship. Francine Alexander had told the interviewer that she planned to spend a year or two in a writers' workshop at an eastern university and, after that, she would go to New York City and seek work with a publishing house to support herself while she pursued a writing career.

Several other students had revealed their future plans to the interviewer, as well. Among them, Rachel Leander. Rachel was described as the 1975 Victoria Springs High School homecoming queen and head cheerleader. She thanked a local women's club for the college scholarship they had awarded her and, responding to the interviewer's question as to whether she had expected her father to show up for her graduation, Rachel was quoted as saying, "Not really. He's been gone an awful long time."

"Ralph Leander," the article went on to say, "has been missing for two months. The police report there have been no new leads in the case for several weeks. 'The investigation is ongoing,' said a police department spokesman, 'but unless we get some new leads, there's not much more we can do.' " Which sounded rather like a contradiction to Tess. If there was nothing they could do, how could the investigation be "ongoing"?

Tess copied the front page and returned the microfilm rolls to the storage drawer. Gathering up the copies of the three articles she went back downstairs.

Jane Leander was no longer at the checkout desk; a woman Tess didn't know had taken her place. Jane had moved to the information desk. She was on the telephone but replaced the receiver as Tess reached the desk.

Compulsively, Jane aligned the telephone with the side of the desk. "That was Albert Butterfield," she said. "He wanted to know if we had a computer he could use to type some business letters."

"Business letters?" Tess said. "He must have a gaggle of secretaries. Why would he type his own letters?"

Jane shook her head. "He said he was involved in some highly secret negotiations and didn't want word to get out."

Stealing another company? Tess wondered.

"He seemed surprised," Jane went on, "when I told him we have two computers for the use of our patrons." She smoothed her already-smooth hair with the palm of her hand. "He acts like Victoria Springs is thirty or forty years behind the times. Rachel says his old classmates are getting pretty sick of his better-than-everybody attitude. Even if he did give a million dollars to the school.''

Tess was still puzzled over Albert's need for a computer. "When is he coming in?''

"He reserved computer time beginning at eight this evening. We close at nine." The telephone rang and Jane reached for it.

Tess mouthed a silent good-bye and left the library, wondering. Maybe the reason Albert Butterfield had given Jane for wanting to use a computer was true. On the other hand . . .

Tess pondered the other possibilities as she drove back to Iris House. Walking along a cobbled path toward the house, she saw Andy Neill and an older officer in the backyard near the gazebo. Had they already searched the house and found nothing? She waved to them and let herself into her apartment.

She spread the three articles she'd copied on her kitchen table and read them again. It seemed obvious that Francine had been researching Ralph Leander's disappearance. But to what end? Being Rachel's best friend, she must have known everything that Rachel knew at the time. Was this the "problem" mentioned in Francine's notes? It didn't sound right, though. The note had been a reminder to hint at *R*'s problem in conversation with *F*. Francine would already have known about the disappearance of Rachel's father. Leander's disappearance had certainly been a problem for Rachel, but whatever the problem referred to in the note was, it had sounded as though *F* had no knowledge of it.

Tess kept going back to the events of the previous Sunday afternoon's tea. Not just Rachel, but Ted and Barry, even Albert Butterfield, had been worried about Francine's book. Understandably Rachel wouldn't want her father's disappearance recalled for publication, twenty years after the fact, but what did it have to do with her classmates?

Had the police ever picked up Leander's trail? She

wished she'd thought to ask Jane when she was at the library.

She made a sandwich and started coffee brewing. A few minutes later, she heard Butts talking to another man in the foyer. "Amateurs," he said. "They erase the computer disk and leave something like this for us to find." There was a loud pounding on Tess's apartment door. "Police, Miss Darcy. Open up!"

When Tess opened the door, Butts held up an ancient-looking, rumpled white sack and asked triumphantly, "Care to explain this?"

"What is it?"

"Rat poison, Miss Darcy. Chock full of strychnine. You told me there was no strychnine on the premises."

Tess's heart turned over. "I didn't know there was."

Officer Neill, standing a few steps behind him, looked at her sheepishly from behind his falling sand-colored hair.

Tess stared at the sack in Butts's hand. How could there have been rat poison around without her knowing it? Would Butts stoop so low as to plant evidence on her property? No, Butts might resent her, but he wouldn't plant evidence.

"Where did you get that?"

"Neill found it in the gardener's shed." The shed was a small ivy-covered structure that sat in a corner of the back yard.

Neill nodded an affirmation and tugged at one protruding ear. "On the top shelf. Right in front."

"I'm shocked," Tess exclaimed.

"You trying to tell me you didn't know that rat poison was there?"

"Of course I didn't. Would I have given you permission to search if I had? I've been in the gardener's shed several times, but I never noticed it."

"Hmmph," snorted Butts. "It's evidence. I'm confiscating it."

"Good," Tess retorted. "If I'd known it was there, I'd have gotten rid of it long ago."

"Another thing," Butts said. "Somebody got in Francine Alexander's room and got rid of that book she was writing. Neill here knows computers. He says there's nothing at all on that one upstairs."

"Really?"

"Really, Miss Darcy. You got any idea who might have done it?"

"None at all," Tess said truthfully. "And why don't you call me Tess." She was getting pretty tired of being called Miss Darcy every other breath. "By the way, I did remember more about that cup of punch Adeline handed me. I'm sure it's not the one I gave Francine."

Butts raked her with his beady eyes, turned on his heel and clomped across the glazed tile floor of the foyer. Neill hesitated, then started to follow him out.

"Wait a minute, Andy," Tess hissed. He halted. "I just thought of something else. While I was at the library this afternoon, Albert Butterfield reserved one of their computers for eight o'clock tonight. I thought you might want to know why he needs a computer."

Neill gave her a puzzled look. "I don't know . . . Wait a minute. I'll call the chief back."

"No!" Tess said urgently. "You know how the chief is. He'll probably think I'm trying to stick my nose in his business to call attention to myself."

"Aw, Miss Darcy, he ain't as bad as he acts sometimes."

"I don't know how you put up with him," Tess said in a confidential tone. "He doesn't give you enough credit for the fine work you do."

Neill blushed rosily. "Well, he wants me to follow instructions and not take any initiative. He says I'm bound to make a fool of myself. He told me I'll make a decent detective eventually if I'll just do as he says."

"Ha! Did it ever occur to you that he wants to get all the credit for cases solved?"

"Well—uh, I guess I have wondered."

Having laid a little groundwork, Tess got to the point. "You said everything on the hard disk in Francine's computer had been erased. You didn't mention any backups.''

''Backups?'' asked Neill as his expression shifted. ''You're right. There weren't any. I did mention to the chief that I thought it was odd we didn't find any in Ms. Alexander's room.''

''She would have made backups,'' Tess said. ''Whoever erased the hard disk took them.''

Light dawned in Andy Neill's gray-green eyes. ''You saying Albert Butterfield did it? And now he needs a computer to read what's on the backup disks?''

''I'm only suggesting it might be a good idea to find out why he wants to use a computer at this particular time,'' Tess urged. ''You could check it out yourself. That way, if Albert really does want the computer to write business letters, as he told the librarian, the chief won't ever have to know about it.''

''Yeah.'' He grinned. ''And if it turns out they're the backups of Francine Alexander's book, I can make an arrest right there.''

''Present the chief with a fait accompli,'' Tess agreed.

''Huh?''

''Solve the case. Why, you might even get a promotion out of it.''

He looked uncertain for a moment. ''If the chief doesn't fire me for not telling him I got a tip.''

''An anonymous phone call, right?''

He frowned, then nodded slowly. ''Yeah. Gotcha.''

''NEILL, GET THE LEAD OUT!'' It sounded like a bull buffalo was bellowing in the front yard.

''Gotta go.'' Neill tugged on his errant forelock. ''Thanks, Miss Darcy—er, uh, Tess.''

''Bye, Andy,'' Tess said.

She went back to the kitchen, poured herself a cup of coffee, and ate the ham sandwich she'd prepared before the chief knocked on her door. She had every intention of being at the library at eight that evening. She would have much preferred going alone, but Albert wouldn't give her the disks—if he had them—and he wouldn't tell her what was on them. But he would have to talk to the police.

She gazed out the kitchen window at a thick semicircle of bright red begonias, which edged a bed of irises, their dead purple blooms long since cleared away and the tips of their leaves neatly trimmed by the gardening service she used. Beds of red and white begonias, pink geraniums, purple and yellow petunias, and orange and bronze zinnias created splashes of color all over the big lawn. But the yard was at its most beautiful in the spring when the many varieties of irises that Tess's Aunt Iris had cultivated were in bloom.

She sighed and picked up the second half of her sandwich. How could she have missed seeing that sack of rat poison in the gardener's shed? But evidently she had. She had gone into the shed only a few times and always after gardening tools; she hadn't been looking for rat poison. English ivy had virtually covered the exterior of the shed, including the window, and the only artificial light inside came from a twenty-five watt bulb.

Tess felt a pang of guilt. If she had seen the poison and disposed of it, would Francine still be alive?

The copies of the newspaper articles still lay on the kitchen table. After finishing her sandwich, she folded the articles together and put them in the cabinet behind a large covered casserole dish. Then she went to the phone and dialed Ted Ponte's room.

His voice was husky with sleep.

"This is Tess Darcy, Ted. Sounds like I woke you. I'm sorry.

"It's all right. I'd just dozed off. Chief Butts really put me through the wringer. The only consolation is that he put everybody else through it, too."

"He certainly did me," Tess replied.

He cleared his throat. "He asked a lot of questions about Francine's book. Somewhere he got the idea that we—Barry, Rachel and I—were trying to stop her writing it."

"Oh?"

"You didn't happen to tell him that, did you?"

"Not exactly."

"What exactly did you tell him?"

"I merely mentioned that you all seemed worried about what was in the book."

"Well, you must have made it sound worse than it was."

"I don't think so. Speaking of that, Ted, I learned something today that might be helpful in the murder investigation. I haven't told Chief Butts yet. I wanted to talk to you first."

"Me?" Suddenly, he didn't sound at all sleepy. "I hope you aren't accusing me of having anything to do with Francine's death. Because if you are—"

"No," Tess assured him. "Nothing like that. I just want to talk to you about what I learned today. Perhaps you can help me decide if I should turn the information over to the police. If you're not busy now, I just made a fresh pot of coffee—"

"I'll be there in five minutes," Ted said and hung up.

"Why did you call me, in particular?" Ted asked after Tess had told him that she'd been to the library and discovered that Francine had been reading the old newspaper accounts of Ralph Leander's disappearance. She was purposely vague about how she had reached that conclusion. Nobody but Luke knew she'd found those notes in Francine's room, and she wanted to keep it that way.

"Because you were close to Rachel at the time of her father's disappearance."

"So were Rachel and Barry. In fact, Franny and Rachel were practically inseparable in those days. Most of our dates were doubles with Barry and Francine."

He'd knocked on her door exactly two minutes after she hung up the phone. In rumpled jeans and a T-shirt, he looked as though he'd dressed in a rush on his way to her apartment.

"There's another reason I called you. You went to dinner

with Francine Sunday night. I thought she might have mentioned what she remembered of Ralph Leander's disappearance. You know, to compare notes."

He looked like he'd been bitten by a snake. "What the hell does that mean?"

Well, well. She had struck a nerve. She murmured vaguely, "Oh, checking her memory of what happened with yours. I assume one of the characters in her book was going to have a father who disappeared."

"Why would you assume that?"

"Because it seemed obvious that Francine was using her memories of her teenage years in the book. In such a small town, Ralph Leander's disappearance must have been a big topic of conversation back then among the four of you."

Instead of responding directly to her statement, he said, "I can barely remember Rachel's old man. Never said more than ten words to him in my life. He was hardly ever around when I went to pick up Rachel, and then he wasn't around at all."

"Is that what you told Francine Sunday night?"

"I said very little to Francine Sunday night," he muttered. Eyes narrowing, he leaned back in Primrose's favorite chair and regarded Tess warily. The cup of coffee she'd given him sat, forgotten, on the coffee table in front of the sofa where Tess sat.

He was probably getting gray cat hairs all over his jeans, but Tess chose not to mention it. She hoped Primrose, who'd taken refuge in Tess's bedroom when Ted arrived, didn't decide to return and demand her chair. She didn't want Ted to be distracted.

Tess searched for a suitably unthreatening question to keep him talking. "You mentioned you didn't say much to Francine Sunday night. Were you giving her the silent treatment?"

"You've got it all wrong. I wasn't silent on purpose. I didn't talk much," he said testily, "because I didn't get the chance. Francine monopolized the coversation."

This was probably true, Tess decided. Francine had had

an unfortunate tendency to run off at the mouth. "What did she say about Ralph Leander?"

"She didn't mention his name."

"But surely she talked about her book."

"For what seemed like hours. But it was all stuff about her vision and her imagination, and blah, blah, blah. She did say her working title was *The Good Old Days*, but she was looking for something more profound, something that could be interpreted more than one way—something more literary, I suppose. But she said nothing about the story itself."

Tess sat forward and said quietly, "Which is what you hoped to learn more about."

He studied her for a long moment before he nodded grudgingly. "Ok, I did want to know if she was putting me in her book. We all did. That doesn't mean we'd resort to violence to find out—or to stop her."

Now we're getting somewhere, Tess thought. She concentrated on keeping her expression only mildly curious.

"Look," Ted said, "I had a bad case of the bighead when I was a high school senior. People were always telling me what a great athlete I was, how I was going to be a college star and a big name in the pros and make a fortune. I guess I started to believe it. Anyway, I went a little wild that spring, drank too much, smoked some pot, even broke into a grocery store on a dare and stole some candy. I didn't even care if the police caught me. I knew they'd let me go with nothing but a warning and keep quiet about the whole thing. I was the town hero." He didn't say this in a boasting manner, but as a simple statement of fact. "Another time, Barry, Francine, Rachel, and I stole an old man's billy goat and locked him up in the high school principal's office. They never found out who did it. I didn't want all that stuff put in a book where my son might read it."

It sounded like fairly typical teenage rebellion to Tess. Nothing to get terribly worked up about. "Presumably, Francine would have disguised the characters, used false names."

He shrugged. ''People who know us would have figured it out.''

Tess had to agree with him. Francine's use of character names that were so close to the real names of the people they were modeled after seemed to indicate the character disguises would have been pretty thin.

''How can I preach against alcohol and drugs to my kid if he knew I'd used both when I was a teenager?'' Ted asked. ''Since my divorce, my son and I haven't gotten on too well, but he's never accused me of being hypocritical. If he knew what I was really like at seventeen, he'd never listen to anything I had to say again.''

He spoke with conviction, but Tess, who had watched him closely as he talked, simply didn't believe what he said. Oh, it was all probably true enough, but there was something he wasn't saying. What he'd left out, she suspected, was the real reason he had been worried about Francine's book.

Chapter 16

From where she was standing, between two tall rows of bookshelves, Tess could crane her neck and see the back of Albert Butterfield's head. He was seated at the computer in the nearer of two enclosed computer cubicles, visible because the top half of two sides of the cubicle was made of glass.

It was fifteen after eight and Officer Neill was nowhere to be seen. Had he gotten a case of cold feet and decided not to act on what she'd told him, after all? Maybe he'd gone to the chief and Butts had told him to forget it.

Few patrons had been in the library at seven forty-five, when she took up a position at the end of the biography section, from where she could see anyone crossing the floor to the computer cubicles. Albert had appeared a few minutes before eight o'clock and entered a cubicle. He had turned on the light, taken something from his jacket pocket, and sat down at the computer. What he'd removed from his pocket could have been a small notepad or scraps of loose paper, or it could have been computer disks. His body partially blocked her view of the computer. Moving to the other end of the biography section had brought the full computer screen into view. Unfortunately, she was too far away to see what was on the screen.

Between her and the cubicle was open space. If

she moved closer and Albert looked around, he'd see her. But she wasn't going to learn anything standing where she was for the next forty-five minutes. It was time to make a move.

It's a public library, she told herself. She had as much right to be there as Albert Butterfield. She pulled a book off the shelf, opened it, and walked quietly toward the cubicle, pretending to read.

She stopped a few feet from the cubicle. Albert, intent on the computer screen, didn't look around. She squinted at the screen. Where was a magnifying glass when you needed one?

She tiptoed closer. Now she could see lines of text scrolling across the screen. Albert must be a speed reader.

An occasional word or phrase was all she could make out. She saw "Fanny" and "Regina" and something about wanting to die, which was in quotation marks. She couldn't tell which character said it, though.

The lines continued to scroll upward. She was so close to the cubicle's partition that if she took another step, she could touch the glass.

She read "—tried to tell mother, but she won't believe me" before the words disappeared.

A step sounded behind her. She whirled around, almost dropping the book she was holding open against her chest.

"What are you doing here?" Officer Neill asked.

"Shhh!"

Too late. Albert glanced over his shoulder, then rose from his chair. He stared uncomprehendingly at them through the glass. Neill opened the door of the cubicle. "Mr. Butterfield? Can I have a word with you?" He went inside and shut the door, leaving Tess to cool her heels outside.

But she could hear what they were saying. "Would you mind telling me what you're doing here?" Neill asked in a deferential tone. After all, Albert Butterfield was a man of power and influence.

"You're damned right I mind! Where do you get off,

barging in on me uninvited? This is police harassment. I'll
have your job for this!''

"Maybe you will,'' Neill said. He stepped around Albert
and bent toward the computer screen. Reaching out, he
tapped on the keyboard with one finger until a new page
scrolled into view.

"What do you think you're doing?'' Albert blustered.

"This has Francine Alexander's name on it, Mr. Butterfield.'' Neill removed a floppy disk from the computer and
picked up another disk from the desk. "I think you'd better
come down to the station with me and explain where you
got these.'' Tess was proud of him.

Albert jerked open the door and stormed out. "I'll go to
the station and talk to your boss! I'll sue you, you incom-
petent bumpkin! I guaran-damn-tee you'll regret this.'' He
paused long enough to thrust his red face into Tess's.
"You're behind this. I'll sue you, too, and take away that
precious bed and breakfast of yours!''

Tess stepped back. He couldn't *really* take away Iris
House, could he? Before she could reply, Albert stomped
past her and down the stairs with Neill close on his heels.
The officer didn't even look Tess's way. By the time she'd
put the book back on the shelf and reached the bottom of
the stairs, they were gone.

Neill had ignored her! She'd given him a tip that would
probably break the case wide open and he couldn't even be
bothered to say thank-you.

Furious with Neill, she drove home. She'd have a few
words with him later.

Now her thoughts were on Albert Butterfield. He'd been
busy that morning. It appeared he'd gone into Francine's
room, erased her computer's hard disk and taken the backups. It was beginning to look very much as though he'd
also gone into the gardener's shed and helped himself to
some rat poison.

The rat poison still bothered her, though. She couldn't
believe Aunt Iris would have left something so dangerous
around.

When she got home, she took out her quilt fabric, rotary cutter, and mat and arranged them on the kitchen table. As she cut two-inch strips of fabric, according to the directions that had come with the log cabin quilt pattern, she tried to imagine what was going on at the police station. Frankly, she would have enjoyed watching Albert squirm.

"Miss Iris would never have left something so dangerous around," Gertie said the next morning, after Tess had told her where the police had found the rat poison.

Tess had poured herself a cup of coffee and was drinking it, standing at the kitchen window, looking out at the gardener's shed. "From what I can remember of her, she wasn't a careless person. It doesn't sound like something she would do. She must have forgotten it was there."

Gertie, who was whipping eggs for the egg-enchilada skillet she was preparing for breakfast, shook her head. "I don't believe it. Primrose could have gotten into that poison. Miss Iris adored that cat. She fretted if Primrose lost her appetite for so much as a day. She couldn't have forgotten the poison was there."

Still gazing out the window, Tess pondered Gertie's words. If Aunt Iris hadn't left the rat poison in the shed, then who *had* put it there?

At noon the Hometown Cafe was crowded. Tess and Luke hesitated in the doorway and Tess scanned the diners, who appeared to be about half Victoria Springs residents and half tourists.

After filling Luke in on the events of the previous afternoon and evening, Tess had invited him to lunch, knowing that the Hometown Cafe was a favorite eating place of local police officers and highway patrol troopers. Luke, who rarely went out for lunch, had agreed because it was a slow day on Wall Street.

Tess had never before suggested that they eat at the Hometown Cafe, which made up in quantity what it lacked in quality. The cafe featured servings of fried and fat-laden food generous enough for a harvest hand. Therefore, Luke had guessed exactly why the cafe suddenly appealed.

"If you do find Andy Neill there, what makes you think he will tell you anything?" he'd asked.

"I don't know that he will," Tess had replied, "but it's worth a try. Don't you think?"

After a moment's reflection, Luke had said, "Sure. I'm curious myself about why they didn't hold Albert Butterfield, after catching him with what sounds like pretty incriminating evidence."

Albert had returned to Iris House at ten Tuesday night, barely an hour after Tess had arrived home from the library.

Luke sniffed the air. "I hope you realize I wouldn't enter this place for anybody else." The cafe smelled like meat deep fried in fat that had been used too many times. Tess could almost feel the grease on her skin.

She smiled at him sweetly. "And I appreciate it, Luke." Standing on tiptoe, she spotted Andy Neill alone in a back booth. "Come on," she said, grabbing Luke's hand.

A waitress set a plate overflowing with chicken fried steak and mashed potatoes and gravy in front of Neill and walked away just as Tess and Luke reached the booth.

"Mind if we join you, Andy?" Tess asked, sliding into the booth across from him and pulling Luke down beside her.

Neill swept his forelock out of his eyes. "Well, uh—sure." He blinked at Tess, reached across the table to shake Luke's hand, and picked up his knife and fork. "Hope you don't mind if I go ahead. I have to be back at work in twenty-five minutes. Can't be late. I'm not the chief's favorite person right now."

"Because you arrested Albert Butterfield last night?" Tess asked.

He looked up sharply. "I didn't arrest him, I took him in for questioning. And I called the chief as soon as we reached the station. He was fit to be tied because I followed up on information on my own." He attacked the steak again. "I told him the tip was anonymous, like you suggested, Tess.'' He glanced at her accusingly. ''I don't think he believed me, but he let that part go. He apologized to Butterfield and turned him loose. Then he yelled at me for an hour.''

''Apologized?'' Tess sputtered. ''But that man had Francine's backup disks.''

''Claims he took 'em out of her car Tuesday afternoon while she was autographing books,'' Neill said.

A waitress stopped at the table and asked breathlessly, ''You folks want a menu?''

''Just coffee for me,'' Luke said. Tess wasn't even willing to chance the coffee. She asked for a glass of water. The waitress was back in seconds with their drinks.

''Did you believe Butterfield, Andy?'' Tess asked.

''The chief did and that's what matters,'' Neill mumbled. ''But I had no reason not to believe him, either. He said he slipped out the back of the bookshop Tuesday afternoon and walked up the alley and down the street till he found Francine's car. He'd seen her leave Iris House that morning with the disks in her hand. He claims the driver's door was open and the disks were in the glove compartment. He said he wanted to see if he was in the book and then he meant to put the disks back where he found them. Swore he had never touched Ms. Alexander's computer, said he was never even in her room.''

''How much had he read when you interrupted him?''

''Most of it, I guess. He said he wasn't in the book, after all. He seemed as mad about that as being hauled down to the station. I couldn't figure out if he was insulted just because he wasn't in the book or because Francine Alexander had told him that he was.''

Not exactly, Tess thought. At Sunday afternoon's tea, Francine had named ''the brainy class nerd'' as one of the characters in her book, but that could have been a lie, thought up on the spur of the moment because Albert had been needling her about her slumping career.

Luke spoke up, saving Tess the trouble. ''Have you read the book?''

Neill looked vexed. "Why do you two want to know?"

"Because," Tess put in, "somebody staying at Iris House is a murderer, and I don't much like the idea of sleeping under the same roof with a killer." Neill continued eating and said nothing.

"I did you a favor, Andy, which led to your catching Butterfield with the stolen backup disks. You could return the favor by telling me what was in Francine's book."

"I already paid you back by not telling the chief how I found out Butterfield had the disks. I figure we're even." Neill wiped gravy off his chin with a paper napkin and reached into a basket for a hot roll.

"I'm sure Tess is grateful; aren't you, Tess?" Luke asked.

"Yes, and if you'll tell me what was in the book, Andy, I'll continue to share information with you."

"What information?" Neill inquired. "You don't exactly have an inside track around here."

"You shouldn't underestimate her," Luke observed. "She has her ways."

Tess shot him a thoughtful look. She couldn't tell if he'd meant to compliment her or insinuate that she was too nosy for her own good.

Luke's blond brows rose quizzically. "What, dear heart?"

"Never mind." She turned back to Neill. "Don't forget, I'm probably living with the killer. I could learn something just by keeping my eyes and ears open."

Neill thought for a moment, then said, "I guess it won't hurt to tell you. But you have to promise it will go no further than this booth."

Tess stuck out her hand. "Deal."

Neill took her hand and nodded. "Yeah, I read what was on the disks. It wasn't a whole book, though. And it wasn't all that interesting, if you want to know the truth. I thought Francine Alexander was supposed to be a hotshot writer."

"She'd been in a slump for a while and was hoping this book would put her back on top," Luke said.

"I don't see it," Neill told them, "but what do I know? It was about four high school kids—two boys and two girls. They drank some beer, pulled a bunch of pranks, stuff like that. One of the girls—she was described as real pretty but sort of moody—sat around and looked sad a lot."

"What was she sad about?" Tess asked.

"You got me. I sort of picked up an idea she'd been raped or something and was trying to decide if she should tell her friends."

Tess studied the young officer thoughtfully. One of the girls had been raped. The pretty one.

"What was the girl's name, the one that was raped?"

"I can't remember, and anyway rape was never mentioned in so many words. It was just a feeling I got when I read it."

"What happened to the disks?" Tess asked. It was so frustrating, trying to pull information out of Andy Neill. If only she could read those disks for herself.

"The chief kept 'em." Neill stuffed a piece of roll into his mouth and chewed reflectively. He glanced at his watch. "Hey, I gotta go." He shoveled in the last of his steak, drained his water glass, and slid out of the booth. He paused long enough to pin Tess with his eyes. "Remember, what I said. What was in Francine Alexander's book stays with the three of us."

"Right," Tess and Luke said in unison.

"So," Luke said when Neill was gone, "Francine's book wasn't the big exposé she made everybody believe it was."

"Maybe not," Tess said, "but she wasn't finished with it. And there might be something in Neill's impression that one of the female characters was raped."

"It doesn't mean Francine or one of her friends was really raped as a teenager," Luke pointed out.

"I know," Tess said glumly.

"What did you think of Butterfield's story that he took the disks from Francine's car?"

Tess shook her head. "The thing is it could be true. He

did leave the bookshop by the back way while Francine was autographing."

"You saw him?"

"I didn't see him leave, but I noticed he was gone. That was about the time that Adeline Wilhelm handed me that extra cup of punch, the one she says she'd intended to give Albert, but she couldn't find him. He came in from the back room shortly after that. I assumed he'd gone to the restroom. Do you think he was telling the truth about going to Francine's car?"

"If he lied, it was quick thinking on his part," Luke said. He took a final sip of coffee, grimaced, and pushed the cup away. "He'd probably guess that somebody saw him come in from the back room, so he could have fabricated his story to fit the facts."

"Oh, he's a quick thinker, all right," Tess said grimly, "and probably a good liar, too. Of all the suspects in this case, he'd be the most likely to have the nerve to put poison in Francine's punch in front of a hundred people."

Luke nodded. "Pretty arrogant, when you think about it."

"Arrogant. That's the perfect description of Albert Butterfield."

A waitress stopped at the booth with a pot of coffee. "Would you like a warm-up?"

"No, thanks," Luke said, "we were just leaving."

On the sidewalk, he placed a hand on Tess's shoulder. "Where do you really want to have lunch?"

"I'm not very hungry," she said vaguely, staring at a passing car without seeing it.

"You sure?"

She nodded.

"I think I'll go home and make a cold meatloaf sandwich, then. I have some work to do in my office this afternoon. Are you going back to Iris House?"

"In a while," she said. "I think I'll run by the bookshop first and see if Butts has let Cinny back in yet."

Luke hesitated. "Ok, but be careful, Tess. I know it's no

use to tell you not to ask questions. Just be circumspect about it.''

"Circumspection is my middle name," she said with a smile, which made Luke laugh.

He gave her a quick kiss and left her.

Still thinking about their conversation with Andy Neill, she turned toward Queen Street. Even if Albert was telling the truth about taking the computer disks from Francine's car, that didn't prove he hadn't earlier erased the hard disk on her computer and poisoned her punch while she was autographing books.

He was certainly at the top of Tess's list of suspects. But did Chief Butts see it that way? Even if he did, Butts was in a bind. Albert Butterfield had just donated a million dollars to the high school. At the moment, he was probably the most popular person in Victoria Springs.

Butts would have to have rock-hard evidence before he gave a thought to arresting Albert Butterfield. Even then, it could put his job in jeopardy.

Chapter 17

When Tess arrived at the bookshop, Cinny and Dahlia were cleaning up, having been told by Chief Butts that the police were finished there. Dahlia had agreed to come when Cinny couldn't find Belva. The shop would reopen for business the next day.

Tess pitched in, too. It was close to five when she drove back to Iris House, making a mental list of the quick-meal ingredients she had on hand. Were there any ground sirloin patties left? A thick, juicy hamburger sounded wonderful. The very thought made her mouth water. She was starving. She'd had nothing to eat since breakfast.

Chief Butts was getting into his car at the curb as she walked across the yard. If he noticed her, he gave no indication of it. Which was fine with Tess. She'd feel better-prepared to deal with Butts if she were bolstered by a full stomach.

Adeline Wilhelm was peering through one of the stained-glass panels in the front door. She saw Tess and quickly backed away. Tess stepped into the foyer. "Hello, Adeline."

"Good afternoon, Tess. Ah was just saying good-bye to Chief Butts."

Of course she was—and Tess was a world-class ice dancer. "Was he here to see you?"

"Oh, no." Adeline glanced up the stairs and lowered her voice to a confidential level. "He came to see Albert. He was in Albert's room for almost half an hour. Ah happened to pass the room while he was in there and couldn't help overhearing them. They were talking about some computer disks. Do you have any idea what that's about?"

It seemed clear that Adeline had followed Butts downstairs in hopes of learning the answer to that question, and equally obvious that the chief had told her nothing. Tess, who still thought the police were being easy on Albert because of his wealth and influence, felt no such compunction.

"The police caught Albert with the backup disks of Francine's book."

"Really?" From Adeline's eager expression, it seemed this was the best news she'd had all week. "But how did he get them?"

"Albert claims he took the disks from Francine's car during the autograph party, to see if he was in her book, and he meant to replace them once he'd satisfied his curiosity. He swore he had nothing to do with the hard disk on Francine's computer being erased."

Adeline gaped. "The book wasn't on her computer?"

She sounded thoroughly surprised by this revelation. But having seen Adeline in her role as Southern belle, Tess knew she was an accomplished actress. Still, she shouldn't have mentioned the hard disk. Tess put her carelessness down to the fact that she was consumed with thoughts of food and, therefore, off guard.

"I heard him ask Albert to sign a statement. Do you think they're going to arrest him?"

Tess shrugged. "Apparently not. You saw the chief leave alone." The statement was probably taken from Albert's interview at the police station last night. To avoid calling him to the station again, Butts had brought the statement to Iris House for Albert's signature. *Another example of the preferential treatment Albert was getting*, Tess thought.

Adeline's blue eyes had narrowed in speculation. "Excuse me, Tess. I have to get ready for dinner." She ran up the stairs.

Adeline's expression was that of a woman who was up to something, but Tess was too tired and hungry to try to figure it out. As she unlocked the door to her apartment, she heard Adeline's footsteps in the upstairs hall. She was still running.

What had Tess's unguarded remark unleashed?

Well, she thought, *Officer Neill himself had mentioned the blank hard disk to her and he hadn't told her to keep it quiet.*

She fed Primrose and then took inventory of her pantry and refrigerator. She hadn't realized her stock of groceries was so sparse. A jar of peanut butter and a few cans of soup in the pantry, chicken breasts and three frozen dinners in the freezer. No ground beef, and visions of hamburgers still danced in her head.

Sighing, she closed the freezer door. Luke was interviewing a potential new client this evening, so she was on her own. Well, she wanted a hamburger and that's what she'd have. With some of Harry's curly fries.

She retrieved her purse from the couch in the sitting room, where she'd dropped it, and left the apartment again.

Luckily for Tess's empty stomach, at five forty-five Harry's Grill wasn't as crowded as it would be a little later. As a waitress led Tess to a table, a woman's voice called to her.

"Tess!" It was Jane Leander. She and her mother were seated in a back booth.

Taking the menu the waitress had given her, Tess went back to say hello.

"If you're alone, why don't you join us?" Jane suggested. She scooted over against the wall to make room for Tess beside her.

"Thanks. I'd like to." Tess slid into the booth facing Coralee. "How are you, Mrs. Leander?"

Coralee's face was drawn, her eyes tired, and Tess remembered what Jane had told her earlier—Francine's murder had upset Coralee so much that she'd hardly slept at night and, when she did, she had nightmares. Now, she seemed to gather herself together with effort and murmured, "I'm all right."

"No, she isn't," Jane contradicted. "She took the day off from work to rest. But I don't think she slept much."

"I had a little nap," Coralee protested.

Jane glanced at Tess with a slight tightening of her lips. "With the emphasis on little," she said. "I made her come to dinner with me just to get her out of the house." Jane's plate was almost empty, but Coralee's dinner appeared virtually untouched.

"I wish you wouldn't fuss, Jane," Coralee chided with an impatient movement of her shoulders. "I'll be fine. I've had these bouts of insomnia before. I'm seeing the doctor tomorrow. He'll give me some sleeping pills."

Frown wrinkles appeared in Jane's brow. "I don't remember you ever needing sleeping pills before. But Rachel says you took them when we were kids." Coralee didn't deny it. "I don't like the idea of you starting on them again," Jane went on. "They can be addicting, Mother."

Coralee forced a smile. "Jane, you're a regular fussbudget. I'm only going to get a few pills to tide me over. Just till—" She looked down at her uncut pork chop and the rice and green beans of which she'd eaten perhaps a spoonful or two.

Tess reached across the table and laid her hand over Coralee's. "Till you get over what happened to Francine?" she asked gently.

Coralee clutched Tess's hand like a lifeline.

"I know how you feel," Tess said, "and I only met her last week. She made a lasting impression, nevertheless. I think we're probably all suffering from shock, to one degree or another. But it's much worse for you because you'd known her for such a long time."

Coralee smiled at her gratefully and released her hand. "Every year she sent me a Christmas card with a note about how she was and what she'd been doing. She's the only one of Rachel's old friends who never forgot.''

They were interrupted by the waitress, who took Tess's order. Burger, curly fries, and coffee.

When the waitress left, Tess said, "I know that Francine and Rachel were close friends when they were growing up. Francine spent a lot of time at your house, I understand.''

Coralee nodded. "During their high school years, Francine was there so much I felt like I had three daughters. Her mother was sickly, you know—she's dead now. She often didn't feel like cooking, so Francine ate dinner with us a lot of the time.''

Jane, who had been meticulously refolding her paper napkin, sat forward. "I remember her eating with us,'' she said suddenly, "gosh, how could I have forgotten?'' She shook her head quizzically. "I don't remember things from my childhood the way other people seem to. At times I think there's something wrong with me.''

"It was the trauma of your father's disappearance, Jane,'' Coralee said, "when you were at such a vulnerable age.''

Jane glanced at Tess. "I was nine, but I can't remember what he looked like without getting out the family album. Even then, it's like I'm looking at a stranger.''

Tess could empathize with Jane. Her own mother had died when she was twelve and her image had faded in Tess's memory in the intervening years. Tess's father had remarried a much younger woman, and they had two children. Since her father was with the state department, stationed in France, Tess didn't know her twelve-year-old half brother, Curt, and thirteen-year-old half sister, Madison, as well as she'd like to. Although she and her father talked on the telephone frequently, she saw the family only once a year, when they returned to the states on vacation.

"The brain is a marvelous self-defense mechanism,'' Tess said to Jane. "It blocks out things that are too sad to remember.'' She paused. "Did the police ever get any leads as to where your father went?''

Jane looked at her mother, who said, "No. He managed to disappear without a trace. Of course, a private investigator might have found something the police missed, but I couldn't afford to hire one."

Jane reached for her iced tea. "How did we get on this subject? We were talking about poor Francine and how she loved Mother's cooking so much. Didn't you say she even copied down some of your recipes, Mother?"

Coralee seemed relieved to go on to something else. "She used them, too—later on. When she was married to her first husband, she called me long distance, two or three times, to find out why a recipe I'd given her didn't turn out the same when she prepared it. Every time it turned out she'd omitted an important ingredient. She was trying to write, though she hadn't sold anything yet, and evidently her mind was on that most of the time. She had a habit of putting something on the stove or in the oven to cook and forgetting all about it because she was writing—until she smelled it burning. I think she finally gave up cooking altogether."

"Maybe that's why she had a weight problem," Jane suggested. "All that restaurant food."

"Speaking of restaurant food . . ." Tess said as her burger and fries arrived. She cut the burger in half, poured ketchup on the fries and began eating. "Did you and Francine get a chance to talk alone in the last few days, Mrs. Leander?"

Coralee sighed heavily. "Last Thursday, before Rachel and the others arrived for the reunion. Francine picked me up at work and took me out to dinner."

"Did she talk about the book she was writing?" Tess asked.

"A little. I've read her previous books. Bless her heart, she wasn't a wonderful writer. She told me she was writing better than ever, though, and that her new book was totally different from the others. Much more literary, she said." Coralee smiled briefly. "She was going to use something from Shakespeare in the title. I guess she thought that would give the book credibility.''

Jane wrinkled her nose. "I'm afraid it would take more than a title to turn Francine into a literary writer. If she hadn't been from Victoria Springs, we probably wouldn't have bought her books for the library. Not that we have anything against romance novels, but there are far better writers than Francine in the genre. I can't imagine how she ever made the best-seller list in the first place.''

"Luck and promotion," Coralee said. "Francine told me herself that her publisher decided to get behind the first book because sales of romance novels at that time were something like sixty or seventy percent of all fiction. And the book had a beautiful cover, too. That was another bit of luck.''

"Did she tell you anything about the story of her new book?" Tess asked.

Coralee rubbed the spot between her eyebrows, as though she had a headache. "No. Just that it wasn't a romance. It had romance in it, she said, but it would never be sold— no, that's not the word she used . . . packaged, that's it. It would not be packaged as a romance." Coralee shrugged. "That must be a publishing term. When Francine was talking about writing, she used some words I didn't fully understand.'' She looked faintly embarrassed. "Frankly, I didn't ask her to explain because I didn't want to encourage her. Francine could go on for hours about writing.''

Jane smiled. "Oh, Lord, could she.''

Coralee heaved a weary breath. "If I'd known what was going to happen to her, I'd have let her talk all night.'' She pushed her still-full plate aside and dropped her unused paper napkin beside it. "I wish I'd been more tolerant of her obsession with her books. It wouldn't have hurt me for one evening.''

"People always wish they'd said or done something differently when a person dies," Tess said.

Coralee forced a social smile. "I suppose.'' She reached

for her purse, which was on the seat beside her. "I'd like to go home now, Jane. I'm feeling so tired."

Jane picked up their ticket. "Maybe you'll sleep tonight," she said hopefully. "Tess, will I see you at the library again soon?"

"I'm not sure."

"Well, I'll see you somewhere soon, anyway." Coralee clutched her purse strap in both hands and shifted restlessly. Jane said good-bye and followed her mother across the restaurant.

Chapter 18

Adeline couldn't wait to see the *Victoria Springs Gazette*. Surely they'd had time to investigate her tip about Albert being questioned by the police and would at least mention it. On Thursday, the day the weekly paper was delivered, she was the first guest down to breakfast, dressed in a soft cotton dress with giant daffodils all over it.

She thrust her head into the kitchen. "Good morning, all," she caroled. "Tess, has the paper arrived?"

Tess set her coffee down. "It should be out front. I'll get it."

"No, don't get up," Adeline insisted. "I'll go."

"She's mighty chipper this morning," Gertie said when they'd heard the front door open and close. She had already placed a bowl of her homemade bran and nut cereal on the sideboard in the dining room along with sugar, sugar substitute, two pitchers of milk, whole and skim, and a third pitcher of fresh-squeezed orange juice. The cereal, a mixture of bran flakes, walnuts, dates, dried apple slices, and banana chips, was a filling meal in itself. But, for those who wanted something else, blueberry muffins, croissants and a variety of jellies and jams were also on offer.

"She's hoping Albert is about to be arrested for Francine's murder," Tess murmured. She had already filled Gertie in on Albert and the backup computer disks.

"What do you think?" Gertie asked. "Did he do it?"

Tess had spent a sleepless hour during the night mulling over that very question. "I'm only sure of one thing. They won't touch him unless they find more evidence than they have now," she said.

"Money can sure come in handy," Gertie observed sourly.

Tess sipped her coffee. "True. But to be fair, Albert doesn't seem to have the strongest motive." Although Albert may not have known that until after Francine was dead and he'd read her book. Tess paused to consider the thought before she went on. "From what I heard Francine say, the book was about the Four Musketeers—under false names, of course. Even if Francine had intended to portray Albert as the brainy class nerd, as she put it, that's hardly a motive—" She fell silent as Adeline returned to the dining room, eagerly unfolding the paper to the front page.

There was silence as Adeline scanned the page. From where she sat at the kitchen table, Tess had a clear view of Adeline, standing at the end of the dining room table.

All at once, the blood drained from Adeline's face. "Oh, dear God."

Tess rose in alarm and went to her. "Adeline?" Adeline's eyes were fixed on the front page and she didn't seem to hear Tess. "Adeline . . . are you all right?"

Adeline's hands trembled as she reached out to hold onto the back of a Windsor chair. The newspaper slid to the floor.

"*He* did this. What have we done to him to deserve such cruelty?" It was a tortured cry.

Tess stared at Adeline. "Who?"

"Albert Butterfield." Adeline's face crumpled and tears trickled down her cheeks.

Tess glanced toward the foyer, praying that Albert wouldn't appear before Adeline had composed herself. "I don't understand, Adeline. What has he done?"

Adeline released the chair back and snatched a napkin from the sideboard. "He has destroyed Barry's chances of being elected." Her face sharpened, hardened. "Oh, God, Barry. I have to warn him."

As Adeline hurried through the parlor and up the stairs, Tess bent to pick up the newspaper. The story of Francine Alexander's death was the lead. The article revealed nothing Tess did not already know. Then she read the headline blazoned across the middle of the front page and understood Adeline's reaction.

Returning to the kitchen, she spread the paper on the center island. "Gertie, look at this."

With Gertie reading over her shoulder, Tess read the second article quickly.

Wilhelm Son in Swiss Reformatory

An investigation by the *Gazette* has revealed that Robert Wilhelm, 15, son of State Representative Barry Wilhelm, was convicted earlier this year in a Jefferson City court on one count of burglary and two counts of dealing illegal drugs.

In a plea bargain worked out with the prosecutor, Wilhelm was placed on five years probation. The defense agreed that Wilhelm would spend a minimum of two years in the Alpine School in Berne, Switzerland.

In interviews with educational authorities in the U.S. and Switzerland, the *Gazette* has learned that the Alpine School is an expensive reformatory for incorrigible youths. "A fancy prison," according to one educator who asked not to be named, "with barred windows and locked doors. Families who are able to get court cooperation send their kids there in lieu of prison."

Representative Wilhelm has been quoted in state papers as saying his son is attending a Swiss boarding school to "broaden his cultural experience."

Was Albert responsible for the story about the Wilhelms' son? Tess wondered. Adeline obviously thought so, and Tess thought the man was capable of such cruelty. "Honestly," she said, planting her hands on her hips, "this is so unfair."

"I heard Mrs. Wilhelm say somebody gave this story to the paper," Gertie muttered. She shook her head sadly. "I reckon she meant Albert Butterfield. You reckon it's true?"

Tess struggled to keep an open mind. "If he's eager to see the paper when he comes down, I'd say Adeline is right." A picture of Albert and the announcement of his million-dollar contribution to the high school took up the bottom of the front page. Tess opened the paper to scan the inside pages. She almost missed a small article buried in the middle of the paper. As she was turning the page, the name Butterfield in a headline set in small type caught her eye.

Butterfield Questioned by Police

According to police records, wealthy philanthropist Albert Butterfield, in town for a high school reunion, was questioned Tuesday night by Victoria Springs police. "He's assisting us in our investigation of the murder of Francine Alexander," Chief Desmond Butts told the *Gazette.*

Butterfield and Alexander were 1975 graduates of Victoria Springs High School.

It made Albert sound like a mere concerned citizen instead of a murder suspect.

Disgusted, Tess folded the paper and tossed it in a drawer.

Momentarily, Albert, in a fresh white shirt, open at the neck, and knife-creased gray trousers, strolled into the dining room. Tess greeted him grudgingly. "Good morning, Albert."

"'Morning," he murmured as he glanced around the dining room and then into the kitchen. "Isn't this the day the local paper comes out?"

"Yes," Tess said, exchanging a speaking glance with Gertie.

"Do you have it?"

"The delivery boy must have skipped us today." Tess lied without a qualm. "Sorry. You can get one in town."

Tess and Gertie exchanged a longer look as Albert left the house, without breakfast, to go to town.

"Does that answer your question?" Tess asked.

"I suppose," Gertie replied, "he could be eager to see the article about his contribution to the high school, though."

The way she said it suggested that she didn't believe that for a minute. Nor did Tess.

Albert returned with the paper while Rita, Rachel, and Ted were at breakfast. The paper was folded to an inside page. He walked past them without a word and straight into the kitchen. He tossed the paper on the kitchen table, where Tess was lingering over a last cup of coffee.

Glaring at Tess, he stabbed the article concerning his being questioned by the police with an index finger. "Are you responsible for this?"

Outwardly calm, Tess leaned over and read the article loudly enough for the guests in the dining room to hear. A hush had fallen on the dining room by the time she looked up at Albert and asked calmly, "Responsible for what? Your being questioned by the police? I think you can take full credit for that, Albert. You had possession of evidence in a murder investigation."

"I'm talking about the article," Albert snarled. "How did the paper get wind of it?"

Tess shrugged. "You'll have to ask them. *I* didn't give them the information." Although she thought she knew who had—Adeline Wilhelm. And Adeline had heard it from Tess. She might have felt guilty for her slip of the tongue had she not already seen the article about the Wilhelm's son, which she was now sure Albert had leaked to the paper. "Frankly, Albert, you should be thankful the paper didn't report the full story. They weren't so charitable to the Wilhelms."

Albert cursed and stomped out of the room, again ignoring his fellow guests as he passed them, and went up the stairs.

Ted Ponte hovered in the kitchen doorway. "Tess, could I see the paper?"

Tess sighed. She could refuse, but it was only a matter of time until everybody saw the front page. She handed the paper to Ted, then followed him into the dining room.

"What evidence did Albert have?" Rachel asked Tess.

"I don't think I should say any more about that."

Rita merely scowled at her cereal. "Maybe they'll arrest him and let us leave this place."

"But—"

Before Rachel could go on, Ted, who had refolded the paper with the front page out, cried, "Oh, my God! Look at this."

He leaned toward Rachel, who sat next to him, and they read the article about the Wilhelms' son silently.

As she finished reading, Rachel took a deep breath. "Poor Barry. I wonder if he's seen this?"

Ted laid the paper on the table. Rita who had suddenly become interested in the conversation began to read the front page.

"Adeline has," Tess said in answer to Rachel's question, "and she went up to tell Barry."

"It seems a huge coincidence that the paper prints this while Barry and Adeline are in town for the reunion," Ted mused.

"They must have just learned about it," Rachel said.

Ted's eyes narrowed. "And how do you suppose that happened?" He turned to stare through the parlor toward the stairs Albert had just ascended. "I'll give you odds . . . That smarmy, little geek."

"Albert?" Rachel asked.

"Who else? He's been cutting down Barry ever since we got here."

Rita looked up from the paper. A black star-shaped beauty mark had been painted on one cheek. "This won't help Wilhelm's chances of getting elected to the Senate," she said matter-of-factly.

"Which is probably the point," Ted muttered. "What a blow, and it couldn't have come at a worse time—unless . . ." He looked quickly at Rachel. "I want to talk to you after breakfast. I've got an idea."

By late morning, everybody in Iris House had heard that most of the large daily newspapers in the state had carried the story about Bobby Wilhelm. The TV networks would surely pick it up for the evening news.

Nedra said Barry, Adeline, Rachel, and Ted were closeted in the Darcy Flame Suite most of the morning. Shortly before noon, they came, en masse, to Tess's apartment. Clearly, the remaining three of the Four Musketeers were, after twenty years, still sticking together in the face of outside attack. Whatever disappointments they'd experienced about how their old friends had turned out were seemingly forgotten.

"Barry's going to hold a news conference," Ted announced.

"We've been writing his statement," Adeline added.

"I've called the Springfield and Jefferson City stations," Barry said. "It's imperative that I make a statement for the evening news. With your permission, Tess, I'd like to do it in the guest parlor at three o'clock."

"Good idea," Tess said. "The parlor is yours for as long as you need it."

Barry glanced at his wife, who reached out and took his hand. Adeline, Tess decided, was the perfect politician's spouse. She might hate some of the things she had to do, but on the surface she was poised and gracious; and she was a support when Barry needed one.

"I know it looks like I was thinking of my career," Barry said, "but we believed we were protecting Bobby by being silent about his convictions. He has a drug problem. He was high when he broke into that house.''

"We didn't really lie," Adeline added. "The institution in Switzerland *is* a school. The students just aren't allowed to leave. It's quite nice, really, and Bobby is going through drug rehab there, too. The paper made it sound like Bobby is in a cold, dirty cell.''

"Facing the issue head-on is the best thing you can do now,'' Rachel said and Ted nodded in agreement. It was clearly a refrain they'd gone over and over in their conference.

Barry's shoulders slumped. "It's a long shot,'' he murmured, ''but it's the only chance I have to salvage my campaign.''

Reporters from the *Victoria Springs Gazette,* three state dailies, and four television stations—from Springfield, St. Louis, and Jefferson City—along with guests and employees of Iris House witnessed Barry's press conference.

It was a masterful display of political savvy. Barry read a short statement and answered all questions frankly. He came across, first, as a concerned father who had the best interests of his son at heart, and only secondly a politician running for office. Even knowing that Barry had spent the morning practicing his statement and the answers to every conceivable question from the media, Tess thought the press conference appeared unrehearsed—not that she doubted Barry's sincerity. The crowning touch was Adeline's tearful appeal to viewers, as a beleaguered parent to other parents.

"How do you think Barry did?'' Tess asked Gertie and Nedra as they straightened up the guest parlor afterward.

"I'll vote for him,'' Gertie said.

"Me, too,'' Nedra added.

What better evidence that the press conference was as successful as Barry could have hoped? Tess thought.

"I raised two boys,'' Gertie said, ''and I know how they

can get dragged into things without a minute's thought to the consequences. Don't matter how good their parents are.''

"Poor, little Adeline Wilhelm," Nedra sighed. "I just wanted to hug her. Didn't you, Tess?"

Well, Tess wouldn't go that far, but she had to agree that, in the final analysis, Adeline may have made the greatest contribution she would ever make to Barry's career.

Tess plumped a throw pillow and set it on the sofa. "That's that," she said. "Now, you two go home. It's past quitting time for both of you." Gertie and Nedra returned to the kitchen for their purses.

Tess was giving the parlor a final survey when the doorbell rang. She looked at her watch and saw it was too early for Luke, who was coming to dinner. A good thing, as she hadn't yet started the meal's preparation.

She hurried into the foyer and swung open the heavy, glass-paneled door.

"Afternoon, Tess," Chief Butts mumbled. But he didn't barge on in as was his usual manner of entering places. He glanced beyond her into the foyer, but didn't move. Andy Neill, who was standing behind Butts, craned his neck to peer at Tess.

Butts looked harried—more harried than usual, that is. Tess hoped they weren't all in for more questioning this late in the afternoon.

"How may I help you gentlemen?" she asked.

"Need to see Albert Butterfield," Butts said curtly, still unmoving.

Tess swung the door wider. "Come in. Shall I call him?"

"Never mind," Butts said as, clearly reluctant, he stepped into the foyer. "We'll go up." He looked toward the stairs, sighed heavily, and said over his shoulder, "Come on, Andy. The D.A. says do it, so let's get it over with."

Curious, Tess watched Butts's broad back and Andy's narrower one as they went up the stairs. What did they want with Albert? More answers to questions about the backup disks? She was still lingering in the foyer when she heard a sharp knock and the sound of a door opening.

"What—oh, it's you, Chief," Albert said.

"Can we come in?" Butts asked.

"I'm afraid I don't have time to talk to you right now," Albert said dismissively. "Is it important?"

"About as important as it gets," Butts said. "Albert Butterfield, I am arresting you for the murder of Francine Alexander."

Chapter 19

"Thanks, Steve." Luke concluded his conversation with the district attorney, a personal friend, and hung up the phone. Over dinner, he and Tess had talked of little but Albert Butterfield's arrest. The only conclusion they came to was that there must be some new evidence in the murder case that had implicated Albert. After going over everything either of them had heard about the case, they still had no idea what it could be.

It was Tess who thought of calling the district attorney. It took a little cajoling, but Luke was as curious as she, so he finally agreed.

"What did he say?" Tess urged now. "Tell me."

"There's new evidence," Luke said.

"We didn't have to call the D.A. to figure that out," Tess said impatiently. "It must be very strong, too, for them to arrest Albert Butterfield. Darn." Disappointed, she flopped down on the sofa. "I guess Steve couldn't tell you any more than that."

Casually, Luke sat down beside her, leaned back and stretched his arms along the back of the sofa.

Tess sighed. "I can't think of anyone else to call."

"Fingerprints," Luke said serenely.

She turned toward him, taking in his expression for the first time. She knew that look—like a kid who's just eaten his sister's share of the candy and gotten away with it. "What?"

"Albert's fingerprints were on pieces of Francine's broken punch cup."

"But mine must have been, too, and probably Aunt Dahlia's."

"The only other identifiable print was yours, about half your right thumb print. A print of Albert's index finger covered the other half."

Tess sucked in a breath. "That means he touched the cup after I did."

"Exactly. They found two other clear prints belonging to Albert, too. They covered up other prints, maybe yours or Dahlia's, but there wasn't enough left to identify them."

Tess was having trouble taking it in. "Have they questioned Albert? What does he say?"

"Oh, he admits to touching the cup. He could hardly do otherwise. He says with the crush of people around Francine while she was autographing, somebody brushed against the empty punch cup. He caught it before it hit the floor and set it away from the corner of the desk. It was shattered later. Francine knocked it to the floor when she fell. Or so Albert claims."

"Does Steve believe him?"

Luke shrugged. "The police also have several witnesses who heard Albert threaten Francine."

What witnesses? The people who were present at the tea Sunday afternoon? Probably. Albert *had* threatened Francine, but he'd threatened Barry, too. He'd carried out his threat against Barry by leaking the information about Barry's son to the papers. Why had he turned to murder when it came to Francine?

Tess jumped to her feet. "Albert will have the best lawyers available, Luke."

"Undoubtedly."

She paced the floor in front of the sofa. "What if they get him off?"

He reached out and grabbed her hand. He drew her back

down on the sofa. "Can we worry about that later, sweet?"

Perched on the edge of the sofa, Tess shook her head. "What the police need is an eyewitness."

"What eyewitness?"

"Maybe somebody saw him put the poison in the cup without realizing what they'd seen." She turned to Luke. "The reunion people will start leaving Saturday. We could talk to some of them tonight and—"

"You've had a hard day, sweetheart." He began to massage the tight muscles in the back of her neck.

Tess sighed and relaxed a little. Luke's fingers had magic in the tips. "Ummm, that's good."

"No more talk about the murder investigation tonight, ok?"

"But, Luke—"

"Do you know how many motels and bed-and-breakfast inns there are in Victoria Springs? Besides, if anybody saw something incriminating, they've gone to the police by now. Steve didn't necessarily tell me everything."

Luke was probably right, and she *had* had a very full day.

He stopped massaging and slid his fingers through her hair. "There, is that better?"

"Much," she murmured and laid her head on his shoulder.

After Luke left, Tess finished cutting the fabric strips for her quilt. The first class would meet next week. Then she put the fabric away and brewed a cup of herbal tea. Primrose padded into the kitchen and yowled at Tess, who took the cat on her lap. She sat at the kitchen table, stroking Primrose's soft fur and staring out the window at pools of light and shadow created by the yard lamps.

If she had to choose the most unlikable suspect for Francine's murder, she would choose Albert Butterfield. She should be relieved to have the murder solved and the killer arrested.

But she wasn't. Something about it didn't feel right.

Albert hadn't needed to risk arrest. He could have taken revenge on Francine in a variety of uncriminal ways, as he had Barry. He'd meant to, indeed may have jettisoned Barry's career. Why hadn't he taken the same tack with Francine? He was probably influential and devious enough to have had her blacklisted with every publisher in the country. And, like Barry, Francine would have been alive to know what he'd done to her. As was Barry. That would appeal to Albert.

Lost in her thoughts, she'd stopped stroking Primrose, who reminded her by pushing her head against Tess's hand. Sighing, Tess resumed stroking. She was tired, but she couldn't turn off her brain.

Something else was bothering her, if only she could pinpoint it. She thought back over the last few days. The book signing, Francine's murder, witnessing Andy Neill escort Albert from the library with the computer disks containing Francine's book, talking to Neill the next day in the Hometown Cafe, helping Cinny and Dahlia get the bookshop ready for reopening, going to Harry's for dinner and talking to the Leanders, Barry's press conference, Albert's arrest . . .

Whatever was nagging at the back of her mind wouldn't come out where she could grab it.

Finally, she finished her tea and went to bed, where she tried picturing restful scenes to make herself sleepy.

But her thoughts kept turning in circles.

Francine's book was the key to her murder, and the book was about the Four Musketeers, not Albert Butterfield. Before her death, Francine had been reading old newspaper accounts of Ralph Leander's disappearance. That had to be important.

What if Ralph Leander hadn't . . .

But, no, Gertie had said that a neighbor—Olivia Perkins—had seen him drive away, drunk. Olivia Perkins, whom Gertie visited once a month at the nursing home.

Olivia Perkins had seen Ralph Leander leave, and he never came back.

Perhaps Olivia Perkins had seen other things, as well.

Chapter 20

It was eleven o'clock the next morning before Gertie was able to leave her duties at Iris House to accompany Tess to the nursing home where Olivia Perkins lived.

Pine Valley Retirement Center turned out to be more than a nursing home. Small stone and cedar cottages and duplexes were scattered over several acres of rolling lawn with clusters of pine and fir trees providing shade and privacy. A seventyish couple were playing a relaxed game of tennis on one of two courts, and three elderly women and a man had an energetic game of miniature golf going.

The drive led to a large, rambling, brick building that housed residents who needed nursing care.

"Olivia's room is in the rear," Gertie said as Tess pulled into the parking lot. "We can park in back." Tess circled the building and stopped near the back entrance.

"Is she bedfast?" Tess asked as they got out of the car.

"She's getting around with a walker now," Gertie told her. "Broke her hip several months ago, and she was a long time healing. Old bones knit slowly."

Tess opened the door and allowed Gertie to precede her inside. Gertie turned to Tess and whispered,

"One thing you ought to know. She kind of goes off in left field sometimes."

Tess's heart dropped with disappointment. Olivia Perkins might have no memory left. "She's senile?"

"Not severely. Usually she's alert and carries on a sensible conversation. She loves visitors. But then she has her bad days."

Tess hoped this wasn't one of them.

Gertie led the way down a central hallway, which ended with halls to the right and left. They turned right. Gertie stopped at a closed door, knocked, and called, "Mrs. Perkins?"

A moment later they heard a thump followed by the whisper of slippered feet on the floor, another thump and whisper, then another. Olivia Perkins was making her slow way across the room.

The door opened. A tiny woman, wearing a pink-and-blue flowered cotton duster and gripping a metal walker, blinked from behind bifocaled glasses with wire frames. She looked to Tess as if a good wind would blow her away. She must be in her late eighties and her face was crinkled with age, like a windshield that has been pitted and covered with hairline cracks from flying pebbles.

As if in denial of her age, her white hair was braided in two pigtails and tied with bright pink bows the same color as her lipstick, which had been applied with an unsteady hand.

Bright blue eyes peered at Gertie from behind the glasses. "Gertie, is that you?"

"Sure is. Came to visit you and brought a friend with me."

She looked faintly lost for a moment. "You already came in June, didn't you?" Her expression changed from lost to sad. "Oh, my, it's July already. I've lost track of the days again."

"No, dear, you haven't lost track," Gertie said. "It's still June and my church group has already been here. Can't I visit you twice in one month if I want to?"

"Oh, yes." Her smile revealed perfectly even, white dentures. "How nice." She lifted the walker in both hands to turn from the door. "Won't you come in," she added graciously. She made her halting way to a much-used Naugahyde recliner beside the room's single, large window, turned and carefully lowered herself into the chair.

Gertie and Tess sat on a small love seat with their backs to the window. Olivia's pleased blue eyes surveyed them. "Would you like some coffee or tea? I could ring for a nurse."

"Nothing for me," Tess said.

"Me, either," Gertie added. "Besides, they're probably busy getting ready to serve lunch."

"Mrs. Perkins," Tess said, "I understand you knew the Leanders."

"Rachel and Jane? Do you know them? Such sweet little girls."

Tess wasn't sure how to respond.

"They're thoughtful, not like most children," Olivia Perkins said. She smiled wistfully. "I'll tell you a secret. Sometimes I pretend they're mine. They come over to see me two or three times a week—when I'm home." She glanced around the room as if wondering how she'd come to be there, and her wrinkled face shifted. "Oh, dear," she murmured with such regret that Tess knew she had remembered that Rachel and Jane were no longer children. "They don't live on King Street any more. And neither do I. I sold the house when my husband died and moved out here, into one of the cottages. I had to come over here when I broke my hip." She leaned forward to peer at Tess. "Are you a friend of Rachel and Jane?"

"Yes," Tess said gently. "I own a bed-and-breakfast inn, and Rachel is staying with me at the moment."

"A lovely girl. So many friends. And the boys—why, I can't keep track of them. But she's been seeing that Ted for a while now—oh, dear. I forgot again."

Gertie glanced at Tess with a regretful shake of her head.

It appeared to be one of Mrs. Perkins's bad days.

"Are you sure you're feeling up to company?" Gertie asked.

"Oh, yes." She seemed alarmed. "Please, stay. I have so few visitors. Are you sure I can't get you something to drink?"

Gertie shook her head. "We really don't want anything," Tess said. "We just came to—" She had started to say "to ask you some questions," but the words suddenly seemed unkind in the face of such obvious pleasure in their presence. "To see you," Tess amended.

"You're very young," Olivia said. "Were you in school with Rachel—no, you're even younger than that. Jane, perhaps?" She seemed to be back in the present now.

"No, I only moved to Victoria Springs recently."

"There have been Darcys in Victoria Springs for years."

Tess nodded. "My father and his sisters, Iris and Dahlia, grew up here. My father didn't come back to live here after college as my aunts did."

"Of course! I know Iris and Dahlia."

She did not seem to know, or remember, that Iris was dead, and Tess decided not to remind her. It might make her feel lost again, just when she seemed to have gotten herself oriented in time and place.

"I would like to see Rachel and Jane again," Olivia murmured.

"I'm sure they'd like to see you, too," Tess said.

"Their father left them, you know."

"I know," Tess replied, relieved that Olivia continued to sound lucid. "That's what I want to talk about. I'm trying to find out all I can about Ralph Leander's disappearance."

"And make him do his duty by Coralee and his daughters?"

"I'd like to."

Olivia nodded approvingly. Tess hesitated, turning over in her mind several questions, wondering which to ask first.

Gertie took the dilemma out of Tess's hands. "Didn't

you see Ralph Leander leave home the night he disappeared?'' she asked.

Olivia frowned. "Why, yes. Yes, I did." She half covered her mouth with a fragile, blue-veined hand, as if to share a secret. "It was quite late, and he was drunk. Disgusting."

"How did you know that he was drunk?" Tess asked.

"Because of the way he was driving." She pressed her pink-smeared lips together disapprovingly. "All over the street. The car came up on the curb in front of my house. I was afraid he was going to drive right across the yard. My husband was so proud of that yard." Her blue eyes dimmed, took on a faraway look, as she sifted through old memories. She sighed. "But he got it back in the street and swerved in the other direction. I watched him from my living-room window all the way down the block." She frowned again. "I suppose I should have called the police but—Ralph had a temper. I didn't want to make him mad."

"Was he alone in the car?" Tess asked.

Olivia tensed and relaxed her fingers on the arms of the recliner as she seemed to ponder the question. "I don't know."

"You don't remember?" Gertie queried.

"No, I mean I couldn't see inside the car. It was too dark. And, then I was distracted by the other car. It came out from behind the Leander house—their garage was in back—and went the same direction Ralph's car had gone."

"What other car?" Tess asked.

"It was that boy, Rachel's boyfriend. He had an old, rattletrap of some kind. I was used to seeing it at the Leanders'."

"Ted Ponte?"

"Yes, that's him. He drove away a few moments after Ralph did. I imagine Ralph had told him to go home. He was always rude to the girls' friends when he was drunk, especially Rachel's boyfriends. They used to tell me about it."

Tess didn't know what else to ask. She looked at Gertie, who said, "Did you see anything else that night, Olivia?"

"No," Olivia said firmly. "We went to bed right after that."

Tess heard the rattle of lunch trays in the hallway. "I think your lunch is coming. We'd better go now."

Olivia's hand fluttered at the collar of her duster. "Must you?"

"Yes," Gertie said, "but I'll see you next month."

Olivia gripped the arms of her chair and Gertie helped her to her feet and set the walker in front of her. She followed them to the door. "Now that Ralph's gone," she said, "perhaps the girls can have their friends over without being afraid their father will insult them."

Rachel and Jane were once again children in Olivia's mind. Tess wondered how much of what she'd told them was accurate. She'd seemed lucid at the time, but still . . .

She put the question aside as she and Gertie walked around the loaded, but unattended tray cart and down the hall. Olivia hadn't told them anything they didn't already know, except that Ted was at the Leander house the night Ralph Leander left home.

They got back to Iris House shortly after the mail had been delivered. Adeline and Barry were in the guest parlor going through a pile of letters.

"They're from my constituents," Barry said, waving one of the letters at Tess and Gertie as they entered. "More than two dozen sent by overnight mail. Listen to this. 'My heart goes out to you and your wife. My son was rebellious, too, and even served time in jail. He's getting his life together now. There's still hope for your son. You have my vote. God bless you.' "

"We've had phone calls all morning, too," Adeline put in, smiling radiantly. "Ninety percent of them from people wanting to say they're still behind Barry."

"The great majority of these letters say the writers are going to vote for me, too," Barry said. Impulsively he hugged his wife. "Looks like we may go to Washington, after all, Adeline."

Adeline clutched several letters to her heart and

laughed. "And that arrogant little S.O.B. who tried to ruin you is in jail. Life is wonderful!"

Tess heard a thump and a muttered curse from the stairs. She went into the foyer. Rita De'Lane was struggling down the stairs with her suitcase. "Oh," she said. "You're back."

Rita wore the same green skirt and black and orange, fringed and tassled tunic she'd arrived in. She even had on the combat boots. It was apparently her traveling outfit.

"I gather you're leaving us," Tess said.

"Damn right. I hope I never see Victoria Springs again. I hope I never see *Missouri* again. No offense."

"None taken."

"Good, then could you help me lug this suitcase out to my car?"

After watching Rita drive away with a screech of rubber, Tess went back to the house and found Nedra in the upstairs hall. "We can get the Arctic Fancy Room ready for a new occupant," Tess said. "Rita has gone."

"Saw her," Nedra said. "Came out of that room with her suitcase, snorting and cussing like people talk in movies nowadays. Never thought I'd hear such language in Victoria Springs."

"Some people in Springfield wanted me to let them know if we had another opening before the weekend," Tess said. "I'd better go and call them."

"I cleaned the Cliffs of Dover Room," Nedra said. "Hope that's all right, now the police got the murderer."

"Good. I'll need it for a guest who's arriving tomorrow."

"Put Miss Alexander's clothes in her suitcase," Nedra said. "Didn't know what to do with the computer and them books."

Tess had forgotten about Francine's belongings. She had expected to hear from her relatives by now. Luke had told Tess that Francine's lawyer had called the police and asked that the body be sent to New York for burial. Francine's parents were dead, and she had no siblings. Maybe there were no other relatives who cared enough to worry about her belongings.

"Thanks for reminding me, Nedra. I'll store Francine's things in my apartment until I learn what should be done with them. May I borrow your master key?"

Nedra pulled the key on a long purple ribbon from her pocket and handed it to Tess. "Gonna do the Carnaby Room now. Reckon you can rent it, too. Don't expect Butterfield will be back."

Tess frowned. She still felt unsettled about Albert's arrest. "We'll wait a few days on that."

"Huh? They ain't lettin' him go, are they?"

"I really don't know," Tess said.

Nedra was disappearing into the Carnaby Room as Tess fitted the master key into the lock of the Cliffs of Dover Room.

The room smelled of the lemon-scented furniture polish Nedra used, and every surface shone like glass. Francine's suitcase sat beside the bed; her laptop and books were still on the table she'd used as a desk. The scraps of paper containing her notes were gone. What the police hadn't confiscated as potential evidence, Nedra had thrown away.

Tess closed the computer's hinged screen, turning the computer case into what looked like an attache case complete with handle. She stacked the dictionary, thesaurus and Bartlett's on top of it. As she picked up the lot, she noticed a scrap of paper the police must have missed sticking out of *Bartlett's Familiar Quotations*. She set the load down and opened the book to the marked page. The paper was the one she'd seen earlier when she and Luke searched the room. Once again, she read the quotations Francine had written on the paper:

Umpire of Men's Miseries
New-Risen From a Dream
Empty Tigers
Call Back Yesterday
Little Wrongs

The paper had been marking the section in Bartlett's containing quotations from Shakespeare. She didn't remember noticing that before, but she knew she had replaced the paper at the same page where she'd found it.

She must have glanced at "Shakespeare" at the top of the page and then dismissed it, but it had remained in her subconscious, for now she knew what had been nagging at her last night. Coralee Leander, who'd had dinner with Francine the previous Thursday, more than a week ago now, had said that Francine told her she was going to use a quote from Shakespeare as a title for her new book. But Ted Ponte had had dinner with Francine Sunday evening, three days later. Francine had told him that her working title was *The Good Old Days* and that she was still trying to come up with the actual title.

How could Francine have told Coralee that she was using something from Shakespeare on Thursday when, according to Ted, she was still at sea about the title on Sunday evening? Maybe Francine hadn't told Coralee any such thing. Maybe Coralee had seen these notes, and then forgot where she'd learned about the Shakespeare connection.

And there was only one way Coralee could have seen the notes.

Tess's heart was racing. She told herself to slow down. Coralee's casual remark about Shakespeare didn't prove she'd broken in Francine's room to erase the computer's hard disk. But it was a loose thread that Tess wanted tied up.

She carried Francine's things downstairs and stored them in her spare bedroom closet. It was twelve-thirty. She grabbed her purse. If she hurried, she might catch Coralee as she returned to work at City Hall after lunch.

As she stepped into the foyer, Rachel was about to go out the front door. "Have you heard about all the support Barry's getting from the voters?" Tess asked.

Rachel's knitted brow cleared. "Yes, isn't it great?"

"Yes, indeed."

"Where are you off to?"

"I'm going to town to see your mother."

The wrinkles returned to Rachel's forehead. "Mother? Why?"

"Just something I need to ask her."

"Well, she's not at City Hall. She took off work again today. She has to be very sick to miss work. I'm going to the apartment right now to check on her. Jane just called. She's worried about Mother. She's not answering the phone. Jane intended to go home during her lunch hour, but they got busy at the library and she couldn't get away."

"Mind if I tag along?" Tess asked.

Rachel hesitated only briefly. "Sure, why not."

They decided to take Tess's car. As they drove, Rachel said musingly, "I'm as worried about Mother as Jane is."

"Oh?"

"She's taking sleeping pills and that concerns me. Years ago, she had a problem with barbiturates."

"The last time I saw her, she mentioned that she was going to ask the doctor for a few pills. I didn't know she'd had a problem in the past," Tess said.

Rachel sighed and laid her head back against the seat. "Few people do. It's not something you go around broadcasting."

Tess glanced at her, concerned. Rachel seemed to be carrying a heavy weight of worry. "What about you?" she asked. "How are you dealing with Francine's death?"

"I've accepted it," Rachel said. "Actually, I've been so worried about Mother and Jane that I haven't had time to think about it much."

"Jane?"

Rachel lifted her head, combed slender fingers through her softly waving hair. She didn't respond for a long moment. Then, "She's been having nightmares."

"Because of the murder?" Tess felt Rachel's eyes on her and glanced from the road to find Rachel staring at her intently.

"What mur—" Rachel halted abruptly.

"Jane told me that Francine was very kind to her when she was a child."

"Oh." Rachel looked away. "Francine's murder. You see what I mean? I've been so preoccupied with Mother and Jane that I've virtually put Francine's death out of my mind."

"People often deny unpleasant things at first, until they're ready to cope with them."

"Yes, I guess that's what I'm doing," Rachel murmured. She laid her head back on the seat again and closed her eyes. After a few moments, she said, "I heard Albert's Chicago lawyers got into town this morning. Do you think they'll get him out on bail?"

"Possibly," Tess said.

They made the remainder of the drive in silence. The Leanders's apartment was on the ground floor of a plain, brick two-story fourplex three blocks from Main Street. The hallway was dimly lighted and smelled musty.

Rachel knocked and they waited. After a few moments, Rachel knocked louder. "Mother," she called. "It's Rachel." After knocking a third time, she unzipped her purse and began rummaging through it. "She's probably taken a sleeping pill. I've got a key here somewhere." Finally, she pulled out a billfold and a small cosmetics bag and held them in the crook of her bent arm while she searched the bottom of her purse for the key. "Finally," she said at last, drawing out the elusive key. She replaced the billfold and cosmetics bag and unlocked the apartment door.

The venetian blinds were closed, making the apartment even darker than the hallway. Rachel turned on a table lamp. The living room opened to a kitchen in back and a hallway on the right.

"Mother?" Rachel called. She went into the hall. Tess followed, a vague anxiety gripping her. In addition to the bathroom door, two others opened off the hall. At one end, Tess could see a small bedroom, the twin bed neatly made up with a blue-and-white quilted spread. The door at the other end of the hall was closed.

Rachel walked to the closed door and opened it. "Mother?" Coralee lay curled on her side, her back to the door. Rachel turned on the overhead light and bent over her mother. "Mother," she said softly. She shook Coralee's shoulder gently. When Coralee did not respond, Rachel turned her over on her back. She bent over her. "Oh, *no*." She grabbed Coralee's shoulders and shook her. "Mother, wake up!" She looked around wildly at Tess. "She's not breathing. She's taken an overdose! Call an ambulance."

Tess had already noticed the telephone on the small desk beneath a window. She snatched up the receiver and dialed 911. "Rachel, what's the address here?" It seemed like a full minute before the frantic Rachel could remember. Tess repeated the address to the operator and was assured that an ambulance was on the way. Turning her back to Rachel, Tess directed the operator to notify the police, also. As she hung up the phone, her gaze fell on the handwritten note that lay on the desk.

Rachel had pulled her mother to a sitting position. Coralee's head flopped to one side. "She's so cold," Rachel wailed. She gathered her mother into her arms.

Tess bent over the note and read:

I can't let innocent people suffer for my actions any longer. Albert Butterfield didn't kill Francine Alexander. I did. I put rat poison from a sack I've had for years in her punch. I had the poison in a pill bottle and leaned over the desk to talk to Francine, hiding the cup from her view as I poured in the poison. I left the sack containing the rest of the poison in Tess Darcy's gardener's shed. I only wanted to get rid of the poison. I didn't think the police would find it. I never meant to cause trouble for the people in Iris House. Francine was going to reveal a terrible secret that would have destroyed several lives. I couldn't let that happen. I killed her to protect my

*daughter, whom I failed to protect in the past. Rachel
and Jane, please forgive me.*

CORALEE L.

Tess looked up. Rachel still held her mother in her arms;
she was weeping quietly.

"Rachel," Tess said gently.

She looked around. "I knew she'd accidentally take too
many pills some day," she choked out.

Tess extended the note. "It wasn't an accident."

Rachel laid her mother gently back on the bed and took
the note. Tess watched her read it, watched as she grew
deathly pale and as grief gave place to horror. "No," she
whispered. She looked at Tess then and somehow Tess
knew that if she hadn't been there, Rachel would have destroyed the note. "We'll have to call the police." It
sounded like more of a question than a statement.

"They're on the way," Tess said.

Rachel sank down on the side of the bed as if she no
longer had the strength to remain upright.

Chief Butts arrived as the ambulance attendants were
loading Coralee on a stretcher. They'd made valiant at-
tempts to revive her, but Tess thought they'd known all
along it was to no avail. Coralee had probably been dead
for an hour or more.

Rachel, who had somehow gathered herself together
when the ambulance arrived, started to follow the attendants from the apartment. Butts stopped her. "Miz Waller,
I'll have to ask you a few questions before you go." He
gave Tess a hard look. "In private."

Rachel looked alarmed. "No! I want Tess to stay. I—
I'll feel better, having a woman with me." She sat down
on the sofa in the living room. Tess sat beside her.

Chief Butts brandished the suicide note. "She says she
killed Francine Alexander to protect her daughter. That
you?"

Rachel's hands gripped each other in her lap, and she bowed her head. "I—I don't know what she meant. She wasn't herself, she—"

"Miz Waller," Butts growled, "we can do this here or at the station. Which will it be?"

Rachel's head came up. She clutched the arm of the sofa with one hand, and her gaze darted around the room as though seeking an escape route

Her obvious terror seemed to touch even Butts. "Nobody's going to hurt you, ma'am. Do you want to call a lawyer?"

"I don't think so—no." She threw a frightened glance in Tess's direction.

"Just answer honestly, Rachel," Tess said quietly. She had a strong suspicion what the "terrible secret" was that Coralee had committed murder to keep hidden. "It has to come out now."

"Are you the daughter she was protecting?" Butts asked again.

With an anguished look, Rachel murmured, "Yes."

"And the secret she talks about in her note had to do with you?"

Rachel looked at Tess, who nodded encouragingly. "Yes," she whispered.

Butts scowled. "You're gonna have to tell me what it was, Miz Waller. What could be so bad your mother would commit murder and suicide to keep it quiet?"

Rachel covered her face with her hands. "I can't," she cried. "I can't talk about it."

Butts heaved a sigh. "Miz Waller—" he began.

"Shall I tell him, Rachel?" Tess asked.

Rachel dropped her hands and stared at Tess. "How could you know?"

"Good question," Butts barked. "How do you know, Tess, *if* you know?"

Tess thought about how to phrase her answer before she spoke. She didn't want to get Andy Neill in trouble. "Francine said enough about her book for me to realize that it concerned her own high school years, and that she and her friends—Rachel Leander, Ted Ponte, and Barry Wilhelm—were the major characters. Something else she said made me think that the character who was really Rachel, under another name, had been raped. Since Francine was researching old newspaper accounts of Ralph Leander's disappearance, I know that figured in the story, too.'' She looked at Rachel. There was no way to soften the words. ''You were sexually abused by your father, weren't you, Rachel?''

Rachel slumped back on the sofa and covered her face again. After a long moment, she murmured, ''Yes. I—I tried to tell Mother, but she didn't want to·hear it. Every time I brought it up, she'd take another pill.''

''So, that's what she means by failing to protect you in the past,'' Butts observed.

Rachel mumbled an agreement.

''I don't know why your father left, Rachel,'' Tess said, ''but I suspect that you finally grew so desperate that you told your friends what was happening.'' Tears streamed down Rachel's cheeks and she pressed her hands against the sides of her head, shaking it from side to side, as if she were trying to squeeze the terrible memories out of her mind. ''I suspect,'' Tess went on gently, ''that you then stood up to your father.'' Rachel actually cringed away from her. ''You told him that your friends knew what he'd been doing and threatened to go to the police if he didn't leave.''

Rachel sat very still for what seemed a long time. Finally, her hands fell back to her lap. ''Yes,'' she said shakily, and then in a rush, ''that's what happened. That's why he left.'' She was noticeably calmer now.

The sudden transformation surprised Tess. Was it such a relief to finally have the terrible secret out? Or was the truth even worse than Tess had imagined? Had Rachel agreed so readily to what Tess said because it was easier for her to live with than the truth? The rush of silent questions confused Tess. She was sure that Ralph Leander had sexually molested Rachel. It was the only thing that made sense of both Andy Neill's idea that the "pretty girl" in the story had been raped and the "terrible secret" mentioned in Coralee's suicide note. Still, she was bothered by Rachel's eagerness to go along with Tess's explanation. But Tess would have to think about that later.

Rachel was saying to the chief, "He'd been coming to my bed at night for more than a year. I—I just couldn't take it any longer. I really would have gone to the police if he hadn't left."

Butts's expression was somewhere between embarrassment and sympathy. "I'll have to ask you both to come to the station and sign a statement. There will be an autopsy on your mother's body—"

Rachel suddenly bolted from the sofa. "Jane! Oh, my God, she doesn't know about Mother. I don't think she can handle this right now. I have to get to her before somebody tells her."

"Miz Waller—"

"Chief," Tess interrupted, "why don't I come to the station and give my statement while Rachel talks to her sister. She can come down later, can't she?"

Butts scowled, but said grudgingly, "All right. One hour, Miz Waller. If you aren't at the station in one hour, I'll send an officer to get you."

"Thank you," Rachel said. "I—I need a ride back to Iris House to pick up my car."

"I can drop you off on my way to town," Tess said.

Rachel was pale and mute, absorbed in her own thoughts as they drove back to Iris House in silence. Tess thought she was still holding something back, but it wasn't a good time to mention her suspicion to Rachel.

As Rachel got out of Tess's car at Iris House and hurried toward her own, Tess remembered something Olivia Perkins had said, one very important detail that Rachel had left out of what she'd told Chief Butts. Ted had been with Rachel the night she confronted her father. Olivia had seen

Ted's car leaving the house after Ralph Leander's. Was Rachel trying to protect Ted by keeping his name out of it?

By the time she saw Rachel again that evening, Rachel had taken her sister to a psychiatrist, who had committed her to the psychiatric ward of the local hospital for observation. And Rachel was so obviously distressed that Tess couldn't bring herself to mention what Olivia Perkins had said. Besides, did it really matter if Butts never knew that Ted had been with Rachel that night?

Tess set a tray containing coffee, croissants, blueberry muffins, and a variety of jams and jellies on the coffee table in her sitting room. It was Sunday morning, and all of her guests except Rachel had checked out the previous afternoon. New guests would begin arriving later today. She had invited Rachel to join her in her apartment for a late breakfast before Rachel went to the hospital to see Jane.

Since Coralee Leander's suicide, Tess had had time to come up with a few other scenarios for what had happened the night Ralph Leander disappeared, and she'd convinced herself that the version Rachel gave to Chief Butts—or rather the version Tess so willingly provided—was not the true one. At least, it was far from complete. She couldn't let Rachel go without knowing the whole story. Only then would she decide what, if anything, she must do about it.

The phone rang.

She turned to the secretary and picked up the receiver.

"Iris House. Tess Darcy speaking."

"How would you like to go sailing this afternoon?" Luke asked. There were several lakes within easy driving distance of Victoria Springs, and Luke had recently fulfilled a boyhood dream by buying a sailboat and taking up the sport.

The thought of getting out of town for a few hours appealed to Tess. "Provided I don't have to exert too much energy," she replied.

"You can sunbathe," Luke promised. "I'll handle the boat. We'll stop at that little lakeside restaurant for dinner before coming home."

The restaurant he referred to specialized in seafood. Their grilled tuna steak was scrumptious. Some of the restaurant's small, intimate tables were in the open air on a pier that reached out over the water. Tess could not think of a more romantic setting.

"I can't wait," she said.

"Nor I, love. I'll pick you up at two."

Tess turned away from the secretary. She was still smiling when a knock sounded at the door. She opened it.

Rachel, slim and lovely in a white blazer, a V-necked red blouse and slim red skirt, hesitated in the doorway. Sunlight streaming through the foyer's stained glass panels created a pink band across her perfect face, the beautiful mask that covered such tragic secrets. Even now, you had to look closely to detect the haunted look in her eyes.

"Come in," Tess urged as she led Rachel to the sofa. "You look like you could use a cup of coffee."

As Tess poured English carmel coffee into their cups, she asked, "How is Jane?"

"Not very well," Rachel said tiredly. "I'm taking her back to Topeka with me. I've already made arrangements with a psychiatrist there who runs a small, private hospital."

Tess studied Rachel, as she lifted her cup in both hands. "Does she know about your mother yet?"

Rachel shook her head. "I want to wait until she's better to tell her." She reached for a croissant, then broke off a tiny piece. "That may be a while."

"She's still having nightmares?"

"Again last night."

Tess was thinking about another night twenty years ago. She could almost visualize the events that had taken place the night Ralph Leander's car was seen lurching away from the house, as though the driver were drunk—or in a panic. The night Ted Ponte's car was seen following Ralph Leander's down the street. She decided there was no gentle way to do what she had to do. She would just have to say it bluntly. She looked directly into Rachel's troubled eyes. "Does she dream about your father's death?"

Rachel seemed to recoil and her hand shook as she set her cup down.

"I think there's more to what happened that night than you told the police," Tess went on. "Your father didn't just disappear that night. I think he was killed."

Rachel bowed her head and all the resistance seemed to go out of her. It must be very wearing, Tess thought, to live with a lie for twenty years. "How did you—?"

"It was the way you looked when we were driving to your mother's apartment, before we knew she was dead, and I asked if Jane's nightmares were about the murder. I meant Francine's murder, but you looked so frightened. And you started to ask, 'What murder?' As though there were another murder, besides Francine's. You tried to cover it by saying you'd been so absorbed in other problems that you'd forgotten about Francine, but it kept nagging at me."

Rachel pressed a hand against suddenly white lips.

"Your father's car was seen leaving the house that night. The driver was assumed to be drunk because of the way the car was weaving all over the street. But the witness couldn't see who was in the car. Your father wasn't driving, was he?" Tess paused. "The driver was terrified, not drunk. Was it Ted?"

Rachel stared at her with luminous eyes. "It was Barry. My father's body was in the trunk."

"And Ted followed him in his own car?"

"Yes. So he could bring Barry back after they . . ." She couldn't go on.

"Got rid of your father's body and his car," Tess finished for her.

Rachel reached for a napkin and pressed it against eyes that shone brightly with tears. "They took him to the next county. The car is still at the bottom of a lake." She drew in a deep breath. "I had nowhere else to turn. I couldn't wake Mother. She'd taken a sleeping pill. So I called my friends.''

"Francine, too?"

Rachel bit her lip, nodding. "She was already there. She was spending the night. She helped me clean up the—the blood.''

"And what about Jane?"

"Jane was in shock. She was standing beside her bed, still holding the ice pick, when I found her.''

The words hit Tess like a bucket of ice water. Jane? Rachel had found Jane holding an ice pick? What ice pick?

Rachel went on, oblivious to Tess's shock. "Daddy had never touched Jane before that night—it was always me. But Francine was sleeping over in my room. He was very drunk, but not too drunk to realize he couldn't come to my bed. After he—afterward, he passed out in Jane's bed.'' Rachel squeezed her eyes shut, pushing out tears that trick-led down her cheeks. "She was only nine. She didn't un-derstand what had happened. She didn't know what she was doing when she got the ice pick.''

Jane, Tess thought dazedly. *It had been Jane all along.* Coralee's note had said she'd murdered Francine to pro-tect her daughter. She hadn't said which daughter. Tess had merely assumed it was Rachel, as had Chief Butts. Even when she began to suspect that Ralph Leander had been murdered, she'd thought that Rachel or Ted had done it. Somehow, it seemed worse that it was Jane. Only nine years old. An innocent, traumatized little girl. Tess's stom-ach contracted. Oh, dear God.

"Jane never said a word while we cleaned her up and put her to bed. Afterward, she never mentioned what hap-pened that night,'' Rachel said. "She was withdrawn for a while and, then, it was as if it had never happened.''

Tess found her voice. "And your mother slept through it all?''

"Yes,'' Rachel murmured, "the way she slept through everything she didn't want to face.''

"But she knew what really happened to your father,

didn't she? The daughter she said she was protecting in her note was Jane. When did you tell her?''

"Weeks later." She gave a sad shake of her head. "Mother found Daddy's wallet behind Jane's bed. She'd moved the bed out from the wall to clean. She kept insisting that Daddy would never have left on his own without his wallet. It never occurred to her to wonder why the wallet was behind Jane's bed. I had to tell her to keep her from taking the wallet to the police. By then, Jane was behaving almost normally again. Eventually we realized that she remembered nothing about that night. She'd completely repressed it." *Why had she never suspected this?* Tess wondered. Jane had said herself that she couldn't remember things from her childhood the way other people could.

To admit what her father had done to her would have destroyed the child, so Jane had created her own neat, orderly reality. A reality in which magazines and memo pads were lined up just so on a desktop. Tess had seen Jane's bedroom when she was in the apartment with Rachel. It was compulsively neat and clean, and she didn't have to look in Jane's dresser drawers to know that the contents were in perfect order. And, all the while, a reality of incomprehensible chaos was kept locked away from conscious thought.

"Before that night," Rachel said, "my friends didn't know that Daddy had been raping me on a regular basis. Nobody knew. But after Jane—after what happened, I told them everything. The four of us, the Four Musketeers, took an oath never to tell what happened that night. We were all involved in covering it up, so I believed none of us would ever break that promise. Then Francine started talking about her new book. She was desperate to have another best-seller, and we were all afraid that she was going to tell everything." Her voice broke and a moment passed before she could go on. "Now I don't suppose we'll ever know for sure."

"Just as well," Tess said, remembering what Andy Neill had said about the portion of Francine's book he'd read. It had sounded as though Francine were laying the groundwork for revealing the horrible truth. Like Rachel, Tess suspected that Francine had been so desperate to publish again that she wouldn't have been able to resist telling the whole story. Somehow she would have rationalized breaking her promise, probably by convincing herself that nobody would ever guess that the book was based on fact.

"When Francine was murdered," Rachel said, "I suspected Ted or Barry, but never Mother. Maybe it should have been obvious, but I was too worried about Jane to see it."

"Because she'd started having the nightmares?" Tess asked.

Rachel nodded. "She wakes up screaming. The nightmares are always the same. It's night and a man comes into her bedroom and stands over her bed. She can't identify him because it's too dark, but he terrifies her. She hasn't dreamed about the murder—not yet."

"Her memories are surfacing in nightmares," Tess said. "It seems inevitable she'll dream about the murder eventually."

"Yes," Rachel said wretchedly. "I don't think she'd ever seen another dead body besides Daddy's, but she'd blanked that out. Then she saw Francine die in that awful way. It must have shaken her so deeply that the memories started to seep out of where she's kept them hidden from herself all these years. That's why she has to be under a psychiatrist's care. She may fall apart when she finally remembers everything." Rachel grabbed Tess's hand and her fingers tightened around it. "Please . . . if the police try to question her, she'll be destroyed."

"It's all right," Tess said soothingly. Now she knew that she would not reveal what Rachel had confessed to her. "No useful purpose would be served by telling the police what happened twenty years ago. Under the circumstances, Jane could never be held accountable for what she did."

Rachel's eyes swam with tears. She looked up and released her grip on Tess's hand. She glanced away and took a deep breath. "Thank you," she said softly, her voice shaking. She sat, unmoving, for a long moment, composing herself. "After I've gotten Jane settled in Topeka, I'm going to tell my husband the truth. The past has poisoned my life and Jane's too long." She straightened and smoothed her skirt, then rose to her feet. "I find I don't want breakfast, after all. I just want to go to the hospital and arrange for Jane's transfer to Topeka."

She went to the door, turned suddenly, and hugged Tess. "Thank you," she whispered. Then she stepped back, lifted her chin and fixed a look of calm on her face. The mask was back in place. She fumbled for the doorknob, opened the door and left Iris House.

Rachel Waller was a strong woman. Stronger, Tess suspected, than anyone had ever given her credit for.

Does any human being, she wondered as she heard the foyer door close behind Rachel, ever really know another?

An Iris House Recipe

BLUEBERRY MUFFINS

1½ cups all-purpose flour
⅔ cup rolled oats
½ cup granulated sugar
2½ teaspoons baking powder
¼ teaspoon salt
2 beaten eggs
¾ cup milk
¼ cup cooking oil
¾ cup fresh or frozen blueberries
4 tablespoons all-purpose flour
4 tablespoons brown sugar
2 tablespoons butter or margarine

Preheat oven to 375 degrees. Process rolled oats in blender or food processor till ground. In a bowl, combine flour, ground oats, granulated sugar, baking powder and salt. Make a well in center of dry ingredients. Mix together beaten eggs, milk, and oil and add mixture to dry ingredients. Stir just until moistened. Gently fold in blueberries. Pour batter into muffin tins lined with paper baking cups.

Crumb topping: Combine 4 tablespoons flour and 4 tablespoons brown sugar. Using a pastry cutter, cut in 2 tablespoons butter or margarine until mixture resembles fine crumbs. Sprinkle crumb topping over batter in muffin cups. Bake at 375 degrees until golden, about 25 minutes. Makes 12 muffins.

Meet Peggy O'Neill
A Campus Cop With a Ph.D. in Murder

"A 'Must Read' for fans of Sue Grafton"
Alfred Hitchcock Mystery Magazine

Exciting Mysteries by M.D. Lake

ONCE UPON A CRIME 77520-4/$4.99 US/$5.99 Can
Jens Aage Lindemann, the respected Danish scholar and irrepressible reprobate, has come to conduct a symposium on his country's most fabled storyteller, Hans Christian Anderson. But things end unhappily ever after for the lecherous Lindemann when someone bashes his brains in with a bronze statuette of the Little Mermaid.

AMENDS FOR MURDER 75865-2/$4.99 US/$5.99 Can
When a distinguished professor is found murdered, campus security officer Peggy O'Neill's investigation uncovers a murderous mix of faculty orgies, poetry readings, and some very devoted female teaching assistants.

COLD COMFORT   76032-0/$4.99 US/ $6.50 Can
POISONED IVY   76573-X/$4.99 US/$5.99 Can
A GIFT FOR MURDER 76855-0/$4.50 US/$5.50 Can
MURDER BY MAIL   76856-9/$4.99 US/$5.99 Can

⇒JILL CHURCHILL⇐

"Agatha Christie is alive and well and writing mysteries under the name Jill Churchill."
Nancy Pickard

Delightful Mysteries Featuring Suburban Mom Jane Jeffry

GRIME AND PUNISHMENT
76400-8/$4.99 US/$5.99 CAN

Even the cleanest house can hide dirty little secrets...

A FAREWELL TO YARNS
76399-0/$4.99 US/$5.99 CAN

It's beginning to look a lot like...murder

A QUICHE BEFORE DYING
76932-8/$4.99 US/$5.99 CAN

THE CLASS MENAGERIE
77380-5/$4.99 US/$5.99 CAN

A KNIFE TO REMEMBER
77381-3/$4.99 US/$5.99 CAN